THE DILLON PRESS
BOOK OF THE
EARTH

THE DILLON PRESS
BOOK OF THE
EARTH

DILLON PRESS
New York

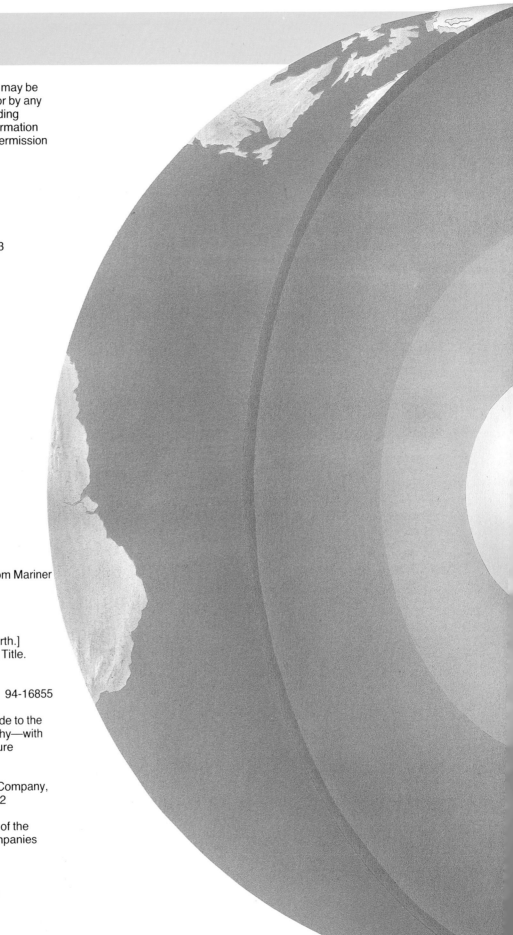

A Cherrytree Book

Designed and produced by
AS Publishing

Copyright © Cherrytree Press Ltd 1993

**Library of Congress
Cataloging-in-Publication Data**

Mariner, Tom.
  The Dillon Press book of the earth/Tom Mariner
  & Anyon Ellis.
    p.   cm.
  Includes index.
  ISBN 0-87518-640-8
  1. Earth—Juvenile literature.   [1. Earth.]
  I. Ellis, Anyon.   II. Dillon Press.   III. Title.
  IV. Title: Book of the earth.
  QB631.4.M36   1994
  550—dc20   94-16855

Summary: A one-volume reference guide to the earth—resources, continents, geography—with emphasis on the past, present, and future

First American Publication 1994
by Dillon Press, Macmillan Publishing Company,
866 Third Avenue, New York, NY 10022

Macmillan Publishing Company is part of the
Maxwell Communication Group of Companies

10 9 8 7 6 5 4 3 2 1

Printed in Italy by New Interlitho, Milan

CONTENTS

Living Earth

When astronauts first saw the earth from space, they were overwhelmed by its beauty. Lit by the sun, the PLANET appeared as a shimmering blue ball under streaks of pure white clouds.

Spaceship earth

In space astronauts have to carry with them an artificial earthlike ENVIRONMENT. Only the earth has the air, water, and food that we need to live. Our planet is like a spacecraft. Without its resources there would be no life.

Life on earth depends on air, water, soil, and the energy of the sun. Without the sun and water, no plants could grow. Without plants to eat, animal life could not survive.

Sending astronauts into space is a remarkable achievement and spacecraft themselves are marvels of engineering. But they are simple compared with the complexity of earth, where millions of different kinds of animals and plants interact in an astonishing web of life.

Limited resources

Like the supplies on board a spacecraft, earth has only a limited supply of resources. There is only so much OXYGEN in the ATMOSPHERE and so much water in the seas and skies. There is only so much room on land to grow crops and to house people.

Earth's human population is growing all the time, and more and more precious resources are being used up. Forests that have taken centuries to grow are cut down in weeks, often causing floods and soil EROSION. Mighty rivers are dammed to provide electricity and IRRIGATION, sometimes causing unpredictable

and disastrous consequences for the environment. Oil and coal that have taken millions of years to form are mined and squandered. Land is cleared for towns and industries that cause air pollution and environmental damage. Rivers and seas are treated as sewers.

Conserving our planet

Every time you turn on a tap or switch on a light, you are affecting the earth. We can all help to make the earth a clean and healthy place not only for ourselves but also for those who come after us.

Nature has great power to cleanse and renew, but when the BALANCE OF NATURE is upset, drastic damage can be inflicted on the planet. Understanding how the earth works helps us to learn how to live in harmony with nature.

Earth is the only planet in the solar system that can support life. It has a breathable atmosphere and receives the right amount of light and heat from the sun. But the sun does not heat the surface uniformly, so life does not thrive everywhere.

Some places are too hot or too cold for growing crops and raising animals. Other places may be too high or too wet. The map (opposite top) shows how land is farmed. The map (opposite bottom) shows where people live.

Inhospitable earth

Land covers less than a third of the earth's surface. Of that third only 10 percent is fit for human habitation. The rest is home only to the few survivors of the indigenous populations who have adapted to the harsh ways of life demanded by the formidable climates.

The CONTINENT of Antarctica is a vast ice sheet where people can live only in artificial conditions, with food and heat supplied from elsewhere. Much of the Arctic is also uninhabited, its vast treeless plains (called TUNDRA) providing sustenance only for reindeer and small, hardy animals. The Inuit people who once lived off the seals and fish that abound in the ocean now mostly live in government settlements. To the south of the tundra are vast areas of cold, coniferous forest.

In the TROPICS the forests are swelteringly hot, with trees so densely packed that even sunshine hardly penetrates to the forest floor. Only the indigenous peoples of these areas manage to survive the difficult conditions. But the people have less and less room to live, as more and more forest is cleared for farmland.

Other parts of the earth are too hot or too dry for much human settlement. Desert peoples mostly live a NOMADIC life or settle with their crops and animals at OASES. More and more have moved to towns and given up their traditional ways of life.

Mountainous regions also present a problem for people. The higher you go up a mountain, the more hostile the terrain becomes. People live mostly on the lower slopes.

Land for people

In low-lying regions, where it is not too hot, too cold, too wet, or too dry, it is possible to farm the land. In these areas vast human populations have grown up. One great civilization after another has arisen. As the world has become increasingly industrialized, more and more people have lived in towns and cities.

Farmers in tropical and subtropical areas struggle—often unsuccessfully—to produce enough food to feed their populations. Two-thirds of the world's people are undernourished and in many places in Africa and Asia people are starving. By the year 2000 the world's population will be about six billion. Conserving the planet's resources and managing farming more efficiently will be a matter of life or death for them.

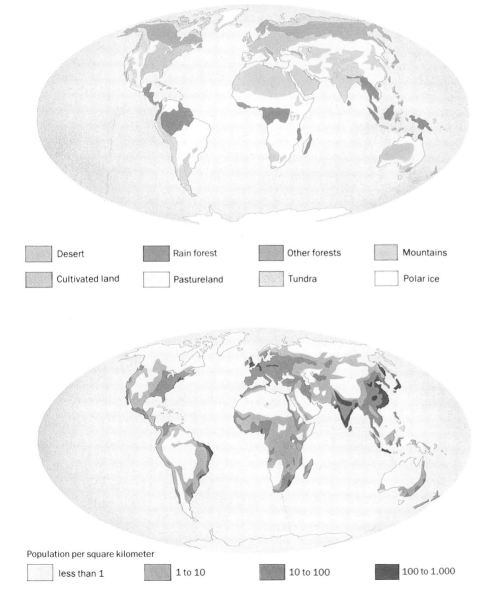

Desert   Rain forest   Other forests   Mountains

Cultivated land   Pastureland   Tundra   Polar ice

Population per square kilometer

less than 1   1 to 10   10 to 100   100 to 1,000

Earth in Space

Earth is a planet, one of nine large bodies that ORBIT the sun. The sun and its planets make up the solar system. The sun is a star, and not a particularly large one as stars go. It is just one of a group of hundreds of billions of stars known as the Milky Way GALAXY.

The Milky Way is only one of many millions of galaxies that together make up the universe.

Light and heat from the sun take just over eight minutes to reach us. All life on earth depends on this heat and energy. The sun is a giant nuclear furnace. It makes energy by the process known as nuclear fusion —the uniting of two atoms. This is something scientists are trying to do on earth. At present our nuclear power comes from nuclear fission—splitting atoms.

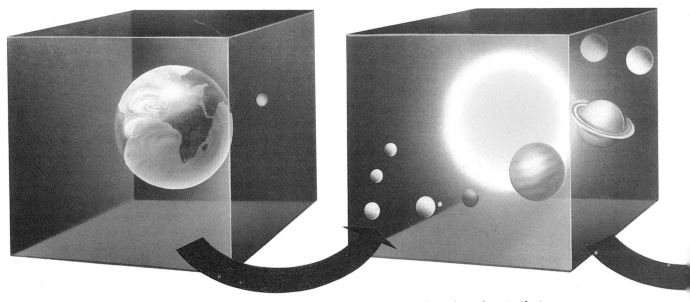

The earth is a tiny speck in the universe, part of the family of a medium-sized star—the sun.

Earth and the other planets that make up the solar system each orbit the sun, at varying distances from it.

The universe is vast—so big that light from distant stars takes billions of years to reach earth.

The sun
Although it is only a medium-sized star, the sun is huge compared with earth. Its diameter is nearly 110 times bigger. The sun's mass—that is, the amount of material it contains—is 99.8 percent of all the mass in the solar system. The rest, including all the planets, is just 0.2 percent. About 75 percent of the sun's mass is HYDROGEN.

The planets
Unlike the sun and other stars, planets have no light of their own. At night we can see the planets nearest to earth because they reflect the sun's light.

The planet nearest the sun is Mercury. Then come Venus, Earth, Mars, Jupiter, Saturn, Uranus, Neptune, and Pluto. Between Mars and Jupiter is a belt of thousands of small bodies, which are known as minor planets, or ASTEROIDS.

You can see six planets with the naked eye, but you need a

Orbit 365 days, 6 hrs., 9 mins., 9.54 secs.
Average distance from sun 93,000,000 miles (150,000,000 km.).
Land area about 57,259,000 sq. miles (148,300,000 sq. km.).
Sea area about 139,692,000 sq. miles (361,800,000 sq. km.).
Total area about 196,951,000 sq. miles (510,100,000 sq. km.).

powerful telescope to see the two most distant ones, Neptune and Pluto. Asteroids can be seen only with a telescope.

The four planets nearest the sun—Mercury, Venus, Earth, and Mars—are known as the inner planets. They are all small, rocky planets. The next four planets, Jupiter, Saturn, Uranus, and Neptune, are giants made mostly of gas. The outermost

know, there is no life on any of the other planets.

The force of gravity
What holds the earth and other planets in orbit around the sun is the force of GRAVITY. This is the force that makes a ball fall when you drop it. The ground—earth—pulls the ball toward it. Every object pulls smaller objects toward itself and is pulled by larger

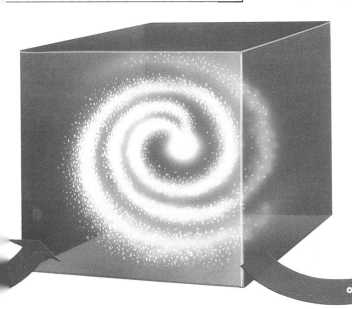

The planets of the solar system form part of the immense island of stars, or galaxy, known as the Milky Way.

The Milky Way is one of the countless galaxies that make up the universe. Nobody knows how big the universe is.

MOON FACTS

Circumference about 6,790 miles (10,952 km.).
Diameter about 2,160 miles (3,484 km.).
Rotation period 27 days, 7 hrs., 43 mins.
Orbit time 27 days, 7 hrs., 43 mins. (*synodic* month).
Time from new moon to new moon 29 days, 12 hrs., 21 mins. (*sidereal* month).
Average distance from earth 238,857 miles (385,276 km.).

planet, Pluto, is the smallest of all. It is probably a ball of frozen gas and dust.

Sometimes you can see COMETS wandering through the night sky. Comets are great masses of ice, rock, and dust that look like big fuzzy stars, and some have long tails. The best-known is Halley's comet.

Every planet has an atmosphere—that is, it is surrounded by gases. Earth is the only planet whose atmosphere contains a large amount of oxygen, which is essential for life. As far as we

objects. There is nothing on earth that is larger than earth, so everything always falls to earth. But the sun is much larger than the planets, so they are drawn toward it. Because they are moving, they are not pulled all the way into the surface. The earth's gravity holds the moon in orbit around it in the same way.

Earth's orbit around the sun is not a perfect circle. Its path is elliptical, or oval. The moon's gravity pulling on it makes earth wobble as it travels around the sun, so the orbit is a wavy line.

The spinning earth

Pictures of earth taken from space show it as a round ball. But it is not a perfect globe. It is slightly flattened at the North and South POLES, and bulges around the EQUATOR. Earth spins on its axis (an imaginary line connecting the North and South Poles) once every 24 hours. It travels around the sun once every 365¼ days. Earth's axis is not upright. It tilts at an angle of 23.5°.

The rotation of earth on its axis creates day and night. When one side faces the sun, it has daylight. The other side is in darkness. Orbiting the sun creates the seasons. Because the orbit is an ellipse, earth is slightly nearer the sun in March and September (the spring and autumn EQUINOXES), and farthest away in June and December.

The seasons are also affected by the tilt. During the summer, the northern half of earth is tilted toward the sun, giving more light and warmth. During the northern summer, it is winter in the southern HEMISPHERE, which is tilted away from the sun.

The moon

The moon is earth's only natural SATELLITE. It is about the same age as earth. Its diameter is about a quarter that of earth. It was probably a small planet that was "captured" by earth's gravity. Some people think it may have been part of earth that broke away early in its history.

The moon takes about 27⅓ days to circle the earth, but it spins in exactly the same time, so that it always shows the same side to us. The first human

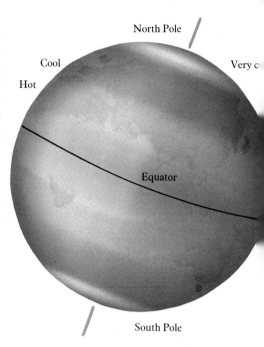

Lands near the equator receive the strongest sunlight and have the hottest climate. The farther from the equator, to the north and south, the cooler the climate becomes.

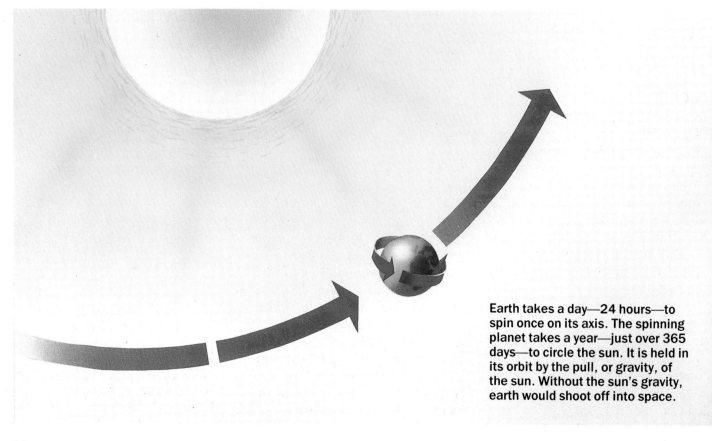

Earth takes a day—24 hours—to spin once on its axis. The spinning planet takes a year—just over 365 days—to circle the sun. It is held in its orbit by the pull, or gravity, of the sun. Without the sun's gravity, earth would shoot off into space.

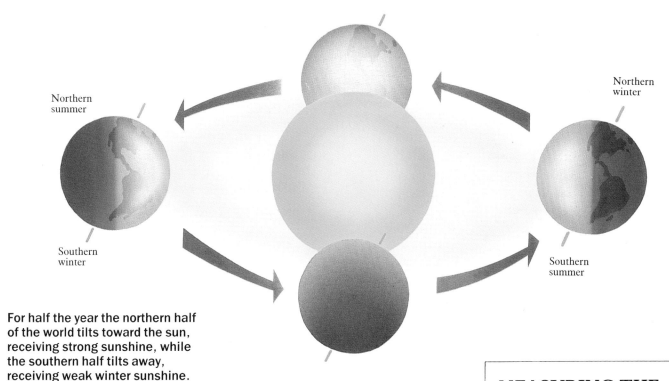

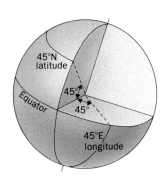

Northern
summer

Southern
winter

Northern
winter

Southern
summer

For half the year the northern half of the world tilts toward the sun, receiving strong sunshine, while the southern half tilts away, receiving weak winter sunshine. For the other half of the year the tilt is reversed, bringing a southern summer and a northern winter.

beings to see the far side of the moon were three *Apollo 8* astronauts who flew around the moon in December 1968.

Unlike the sun, the moon has no light of its own. We see it only because it reflects the sun's light. When earth is between the moon and the sun, the whole face is lit up and we see the full moon. When the moon is between earth and the sun, the moon is invisible. Between those two times we see only part—phases—of the moon. It takes the moon about 29½ days to go through all its phases.

Meteorites
The surface of the moon is dry and dusty, and there is no atmosphere. The whole surface is pitted with billions of craters, caused by METEORITES that have

collided with the moon. Our atmosphere protects earth from similar damage. Most METEORS burn up in space before they reach the ground. The shooting stars you sometimes see in the night sky are meteors, glowing hot in the friction of the atmosphere.

Eclipses
Every so often sun, earth, and moon are in a straight line. If the earth is between the sun and the moon, it casts a shadow on the moon. This is an ECLIPSE. In a total lunar eclipse, the whole of the moon is obscured for a few minutes. In a partial eclipse, only part of the moon is in shadow. If the moon comes between earth and the sun, it eclipses the sun. In a total solar eclipse, the shadow of the moon covers the whole of the sun's surface.

MEASURING THE EARTH

The position of any place on earth is described by two measurements, LATITUDE AND LONGITUDE, shown as lines on a map. Lines of latitude run parallel with the equator, which is 0°. The North Pole is 90°N; the South Pole is 90°S. The latitude of any other point is the angle formed at the center of the earth between the point and the equator. Lines of longitude, or meridians, are measured from 0° to 180°E or 180°W of the prime meridian—0°—which runs through Greenwich, England.

Structure of the Earth

We can see and visit virtually the whole of earth's surface, from the highest mountains to the lowest canyons. We can explore the depths of the oceans, send people to the moon, and dispatch spacecraft to photograph all but ground. Different rocks carry the shock waves and deflect, or bend, them in different ways.

A ball of metal and rock
The earth is a mass of metal and rock divided into layers. If you

the most distant planet. But we cannot explore the hot, hidden interior of the earth.

Our knowledge of earth's interior comes from the findings of GEOLOGISTS who have worked out what the interior must be like by using detective methods and scientific instruments. For example, by measuring the time taken for earthquake shocks to reach various points on the surface of the globe, they can deduce the density of rocks deep under-

cut through the earth, at the center would be a metallic CORE, surrounded by a rocky layer called the MANTLE, and around that, relatively as thin as the skin of an apple, the rocky CRUST, the only part we can explore.

The core
The inner core, at the very center of the earth, is shaped like a ball. Scientists think that it is solid and probably composed of a mixture of IRON and NICKEL. The

Rocks laid bare in cliff faces or in canyons cut by rivers provide clues about the age of the earth and its prehistory. Many rocks form in flat layers, or STRATA. If they have not been disturbed, the older rocks are at the bottom and the younger rocks are at the top.

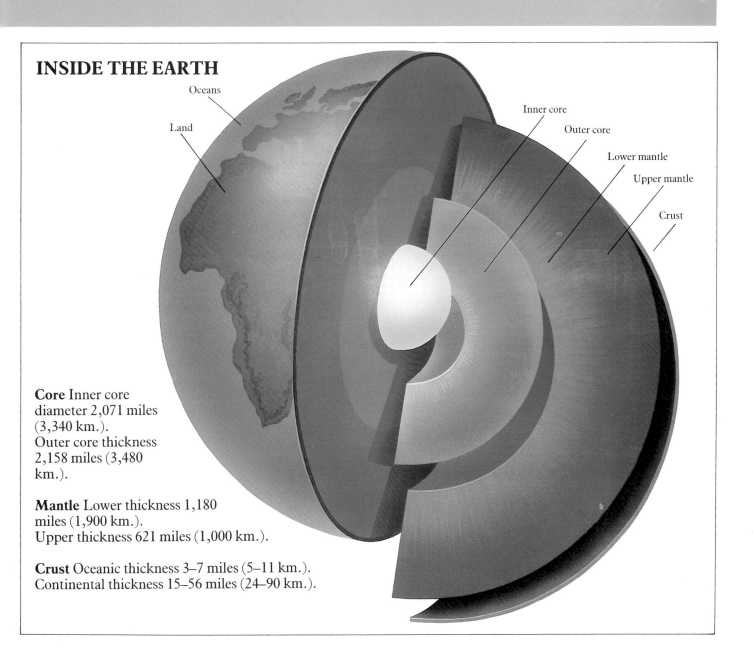

INSIDE THE EARTH

Oceans

Land

Inner core

Outer core

Lower mantle

Upper mantle

Crust

Core Inner core diameter 2,071 miles (3,340 km.). Outer core thickness 2,158 miles (3,480 km.).

Mantle Lower thickness 1,180 miles (1,900 km.). Upper thickness 621 miles (1,000 km.).

Crust Oceanic thickness 3–7 miles (5–11 km.). Continental thickness 15–56 miles (24–90 km.).

temperature may be as high as 5,000°C, almost as hot as the surface of the sun.

The outer core is a thick layer surrounding the inner core. It is probably made of the same materials as the inner core, but instead of being solid, it is molten, or liquid. Scientists deduce that it is liquid because certain earthquake waves, called secondary or S waves, do not go through it, and S waves cannot pass through liquid.

The mantle
Between the outer core and the crust lies the mantle. In bulk it is about four-fifths of earth's mass. It is composed largely of MAGNESIUM, iron, SILICON, ALUMINUM, and oxygen. The lower part of the mantle is solid rock.

A layer in the upper part of the mantle is semimolten. It moves about as a thick, solid fluid, like hot tar. The melted rock is called MAGMA. It sometimes flows from volcanoes as LAVA.

The Moho

The boundary between the mantle and the crust is called the Moho, short for Mohorovicic discontinuity. A discontinuity is a sudden change in the earth's structure. The Moho was first discovered in 1909 by the Yugoslav geologist Andrija Mohorovicic, after whom the discontinuity is named.

Mohorovicic made the discovery as a result of an earthquake in Croatia. He discovered that some of the shock waves from the earthquake traveled faster through deep rocks than through the crust. This proved that there was a change in the type of rock about 19 miles (30 kilometers) below the surface.

Although the upper part of the mantle behaves like a fluid, many geologists believe that the very top layer of the mantle, just below the Moho, is solid rock. They call the crust and this top layer of the mantle the LITHO-SPHERE, a term made up from two Greek words meaning "rock" and "sphere."

Below the lithosphere is a layer known as the ASTHENOSPHERE, literally "weak sphere." It is in this layer that most of the movement between the outer part of earth and the inner parts takes place. The solid layer under the asthenosphere is called the MESOSPHERE, or "middle sphere."

The crust

The rocks of the earth's crust vary in age, thickness, and composition. The oldest rocks, under the continents, can be as thick as 43 miles (70 kilometers), the younger rocks, under the oceans, as thin as 3 miles (5 kilometers). Continental rock is largely composed of GRANITE or similar rocks, rich in SILICA and aluminum. The rock is called SIAL, a word made of the first two letters of *silica* and *aluminum*.

Sima is a layer of heavy rock that completely envelops the earth, under land and sea. The lighter sialic rocks form the continental crust.

The diagram of North America is cut through to show what it is made of. In the West new mountains have formed as a PLATE pushes under the coast, causing earth movements and volcanoes. The Rockies are older, created by the collision of two continents long ago. In the center is the SHIELD, now mostly covered by SEDIMENTARY ROCKS and exposed in some places. In the East, a chain of old FOLD MOUNTAINS shows where two plates collided and the continents joined together. They may once have been as high as the Himalayas, but have been worn down by erosion.

ROCKS ACROSS AMERICA

WEST   Pacific Ocean   Coastal ranges   Rocky Mountains   Stable platform

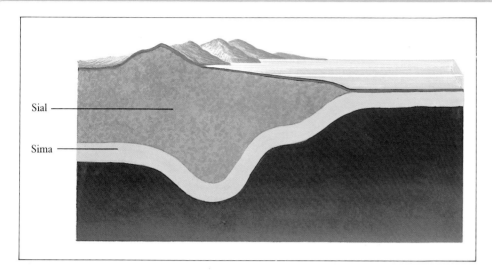

Oceanic rock is called SIMA, after its two main elements, silica and magnesium. It is also rich in iron. Oceanic rocks are mostly BASALT or PERIDOTITE.

The thin crust under the oceans is young rock. Nowhere is it more than 200 million years old. The thinnest continental rocks are 12 miles (20 kilometers) thick. The thickest, under great mountain ranges like the Hima-layas and the Andes, are ancient. The oldest continental rock so far discovered is 3.8 billion years old.

A typical continent is made up of several parts. The oldest parts are called shields. These generally low-lying parts contain the oldest rocks in the continent. Most of them are the remains of extremely old mountain ranges that have been worn flat. Much of the shield is hidden under younger rocks.

Earth's magnetism

Earth is a giant MAGNET. It makes a compass needle point to the north. At one time, scientists thought that it was a permanent magnet, like the ones you can buy. Now they think it is a form of ELECTROMAGNET, like the ones used for picking up scrap iron and steel. The force that produces the MAGNETISM is probably a series of CONVECTION CURRENTS in the molten part of earth's iron core.

The magnetic north and south poles are not the same as the geographical poles, and they move about. At present, the magnetic north pole is somewhere near Bathurst Island, off the northern coast of Canada. Over the past 7,000 years it has been in several different positions, all of them grouped around the geographical pole.

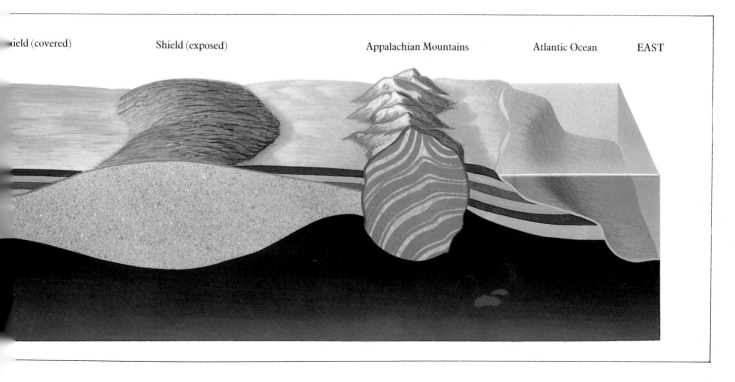

Shield (covered)   Shield (exposed)   Appalachian Mountains   Atlantic Ocean   EAST

Earth's Rocky Crust

Earth's crust and most of its interior are made of rocks. Large areas of the earth are covered with soil, but soil itself is a mixture of tiny rock fragments, decayed ORGANIC matter, water, and air. Even larger areas are covered by water.

Elements and minerals

All rocks are made of MINERALS, and minerals are made of ELEMENTS. Elements are pure chemical substances. The earth's crust contains 92 elements, but only 8 are common. They make up 99 percent of the crust. Oxygen, silicon, aluminum, and iron are the most common elements on earth.

orderly way, making solid CRYSTALS with geometric shapes.

Some substances are not minerals. They include all organic materials that are either living, such as plants and animals, or were once living, such as coal and oil. Water, the world's most common substance, is not a mineral but a mixture, or compound, of chemicals.

Different kinds of rocks are made of different mixtures of minerals. Exceptions are DIAMOND and GRAPHITE. Both consist almost entirely of the element CARBON. Diamond is the hardest mineral known, and graphite is one of the softest. Carbon is present also in all living things.

ELEMENTS

1	Oxygen	46%
2	Silicon	28%
3	Aluminum	8%
4	Iron	5%
5	Calcium	4%
6	Sodium	3%
7	Potassium	3%
8	Magnesium	2%
9	84 other elements	1%
	92 elements	100%

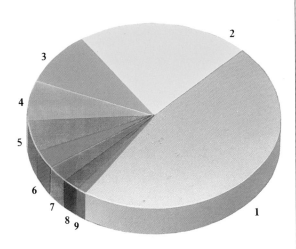

The chart shows the chief elements in the earth's crust. Oxygen and silicon make up nearly three-quarters of the weight.

Some minerals, such as GOLD, COPPER, and SULFUR, are also pure elements, but most minerals are combinations of two or more elements. They are always composed of the same elements, combined in the same proportions. There are about a hundred common minerals, and nearly 3,000 more that are rare. The ATOMS of a mineral are arranged in an

The composition of rocks

Rocks are made from fragments of minerals cemented together. Although there are thousands of minerals, fewer than a hundred make up the most common rocks.

THE ROCK CYCLE

Natural processes are always changing the rocks in the earth's crust.

1 When a volcano erupts, magma (molten rock) is forced to the surface as lava, and new IGNEOUS ROCK is formed.

2 But even as new mountains are created from the buildup of cooled lava and ash, the weather and other natural forces wear them down.

3 Fragments of worn rock are carried away by GLACIERS and rivers to the sea. On the way, they are ground down into sand, SILT, and mud.

4 These SEDIMENTS are spread over the seafloor. Over the years, they pile up in layers.

5 Gradually the layers are compressed and cemented together to form new sedimentary rocks.

6 As these new rocks are buried, great pressure and heat deep down change some of them into METAMORPHIC ROCKS.

7 Some rocks are forced down so far that they melt to become magma.

Some magma rises up and cools in the earth's crust. Some appears on the surface as lava, completing the rock cycle.

The most important rock-making minerals are SILICATES. They are a large family of minerals made of oxygen and silicon mixed with other elements. They are found in many kinds of rock.

The next most important rock-forming minerals are CALCITES. They make up most of the LIMESTONE rock that is found all over the world. Calcites dissolve in water, and there are vast quantities of them in the sea and rivers. They collect around grains of other minerals and bind them together to form rock. They act like cement in concrete. They also form STALACTITES AND STALAGMITES in limestone caves.

Rock crystal is a colorless, almost pure kind of QUARTZ.

The changing rocks
Rocks seem solid and indestructible. But they are not. They are continuously changing. In one place new rocks are forming, in another rocks are being destroyed and more new rocks are being formed from their remains. Most of these changes occur too slowly for us to notice, but some are easy to see. When a volcano erupts, for example, molten rock, or lava, may pour from the

ROCKS FROM FIRE

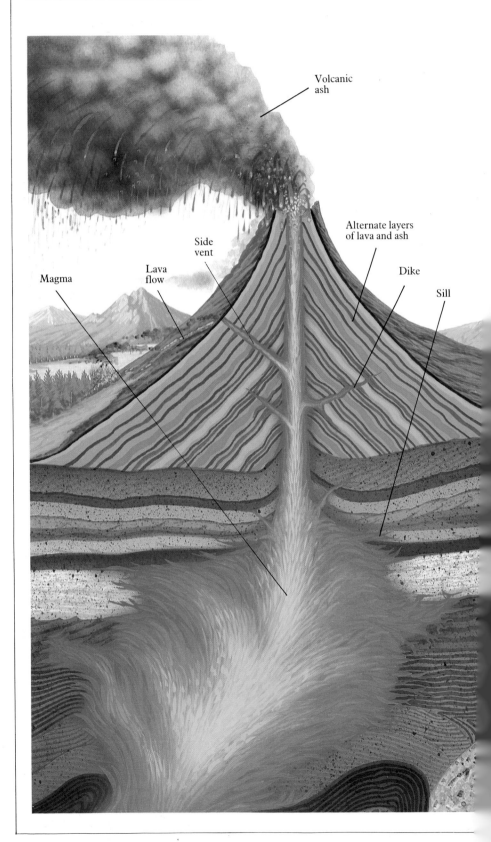

Volcanic ash

Alternate layers of lava and ash

Side vent

Lava flow

Magma

Dike

Sill

When a volcano erupts, magma spurts from the cone in the form of ash and lava. The ash and lava harden quickly to make EXTRUSIVE IGNEOUS ROCK.

Magma in areas called BATHOLITHS under the ground cools more slowly because the rocks around it keep the heat in. It hardens to become INTRUSIVE IGNEOUS ROCK.

Some magma is forced into cracks and hardens into sheets called SILLS or DIKES.

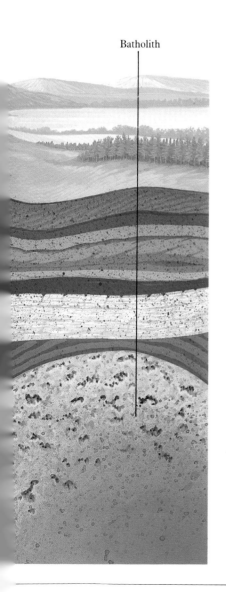

Batholith

crater. As it cools, the lave hardens into new rock.

Sediment in the sea
Other changes take place more gradually. After a storm, the water in a river looks muddy. The color comes from sediment—mud and sand—that has been churned up. Sediment is the remains of solid rock that has been destroyed by the weather. Millions of tons of sediment that was once solid rock are deposited in the sea. New sediment weighs down on the sediment beneath it. Dissolved minerals in the sea cement the loose particles to-

Although made of the same minerals, granite (above left) forms when magma cools slowly underground, so that crystals grow. OBSIDIAN (above right) forms when the magma cools too quickly for crystals to grow, and is smooth and glassy.

gether and eventually the sediment becomes solid rock.

Earth movements
Newly formed rock may be heaved upward by movements in the earth's crust to form new mountains. Other earth movements force crustal rocks downward into the mantle, where they are melted by great heat to form magma. This may reappear as

lava when a volcano erupts, or it may cool and harden into rock underground. These continuous changes are called the rock cycle.

Kinds of rock
The earth's crust contains three main kinds of rock: igneous, sedimentary, and metamorphic. Igneous rocks form when molten magma solidifies. Geologists divide them into two main types: intrusive and extrusive.

Intrusive igneous rocks
Beneath the hard outer layers of the earth is a layer of magma. Some magma rises through the overlying rocks into the crust. Some of it accumulates in huge areas called batholiths. Here it cools and hardens slowly to form coarse-grained rocks containing mineral crystals. Batholiths often push up the overlying rocks to form DOME MOUNTAINS. When the overlying rocks are worn away, the rocks in the batholith appear on the surface. These rocks are called intrusive igneous rocks. Granite is the most common type of intrusive igneous rock.

Extrusive igneous rocks
Other igneous rocks form from magma that reaches the earth's surface. They are called extrusive

igneous rocks. Some form when magma spills out as lava through volcanoes or cracks in the ground. The lava cools and hardens quickly in the air. Because there is not enough time for crystals to form, the rocks are fine-grained or glassy. Basalt is the most common form of fine-grained igneous rock. Most of the rock under the oceans is basalt. Obsidian is a rock that resembles glass. It has cooled so fast that there is no grain at all. Other rocks are formed when volcanic ash explodes into the air. Piles of volcanic ash form a rock called TUFF, while tiny fragments of volcanic ash form a rock called IGNIMBRITE.

Sedimentary rocks

Sedimentary rocks make up only a small part of earth's crust. But they stretch like a thin skin over about three-quarters of the land surface.

Most sedimentary rocks consist of particles worn away from rocks on land and carried into the sea by rivers. Over millions of years these particles are compressed together by the weight of the water above them. They may become buried under other layers of rock.

The smaller particles are washed into the sea as mud or silt. They become rocks called SHALES, MUDSTONES, and SILTSTONES. Clay is a kind of mud-

ROCK LAYERS

If you could drill into the ground, you might find strata like these beneath your feet.

1 Under the soil, you might find a layer of CONGLOMERATE, formed on an ancient beach.

2 Below it, a layer of sandstone, formed when the sea level was higher, because sandstones are formed in offshore waters.

3 A layer of shale, formed from silt in deeper water (another change in sea level).

4 A layer of limestone, formed on a deep seabed.

ROCKS FROM THE SEA

WEATHERING and erosion play an important part in the formation of sedimentary rocks. Rain helps to break up rocks, and rivers carry worn material,

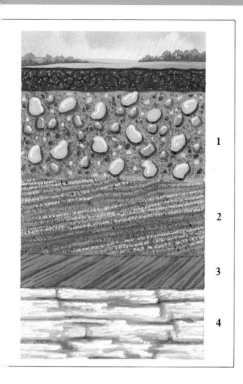

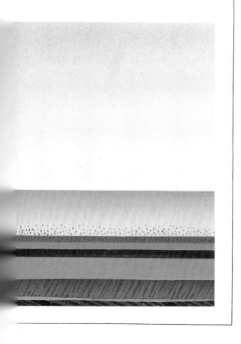

ranging in size from pebbles to sand (far right) and fine clay, into the sea, where they eventually form new layers of rock. Winds also play their part by loosening sand and dust and blowing them across the land.

stone. Sand grains are also washed into the sea. They are larger than mud and silt. They consist mostly of the mineral quartz. When compressed and cemented together, they form sandstone. Some sedimentary rocks look like pebbles cemented together. They are called conglomerates.

Another type of sedimentary rock consists of minerals left behind when ancient seas or lakes dried up. GYPSUM (the main ingredient of plaster) and rock salt were formed this way.

Rocks from living things

Some rocks are made of the remains of living things. Limestone and chalk are formed from the shells of billions of tiny sea creatures. One kind of limestone is called oolitic limestone. *Oolitic* means "egg-stone"; the grains in the rock look like fish eggs. This kind of rock forms when hard particles (sand or fragments of shell) become coated with layers of calcite and are cemented together.

Coal is a kind of rock. It consists of layer upon layer of dead plant material that has been compressed and hardened into rock over millions of years. Like graphite and diamonds, it is mostly carbon.

Strata

Rocks are laid down in layers, called strata. As a rule the upper layers are the younger rocks, but when earthquakes and pressure make rocks fold, a lower layer may be moved above an upper layer. Geologists can tell a lot about the history of the earth from the sequence of rocks in any particular area. They can tell the

age of the rocks from the FOSSILS they find preserved in them.

Metamorphic rocks

Metamorphic rocks are rocks that have been changed. They were originally igneous or sedimentary rocks, but pressure and heat have altered them in appearance, and often changed their chemical makeup, too.

Pressure is caused when a layer of rock is buried under newer layers or squeezed as a result of earth movements. Metamorphism produced in this way is called dynamic metamorphism.

Much of the heat that transforms rocks comes from magma that is squeezed upward through

the crust. The surrounding rocks are "cooked" and so changed. This process is called contact metamorphism. The rocks may be metamorphosed for a distance of 1–2 miles (2–3 kilometers) around large bodies of magma.

Sometimes minerals in metamorphic rocks are recrystallized to form new minerals. GARNETS, red semiprecious stones much used in jewelry, are crystals often found in schists and gneisses created during metamorphism.

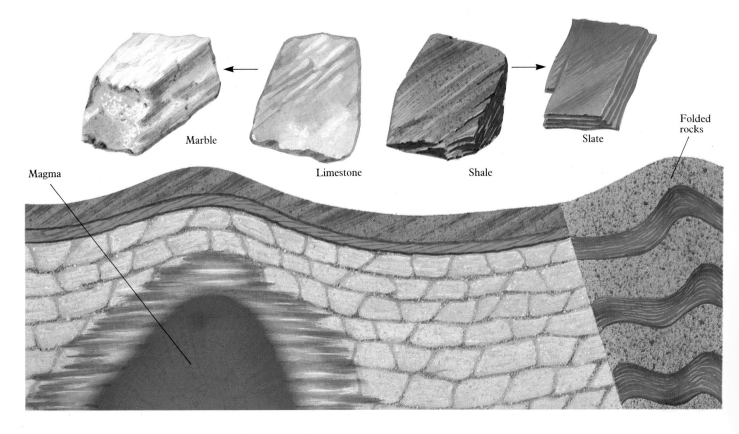

Marble

Magma

Limestone

Shale

Slate

Folded rocks

Often, especially during mountain building, heat and pressure combine to cause regional metamorphism. The effect of regional metamorphism may be felt for hundreds of miles.

Examples of metamorphic rocks include MARBLE, which is formed when limestone, or a similar rock called DOLOMITE, is changed through contact or regional metamorphism. SLATE is produced by pressure on clays or shales. Other metamorphic rocks include GNEISS, HORNFELS, QUARTZITE, and SCHIST.

Metals from rocks
Many minerals are metals. Most are not pure elements like gold and SILVER, but are found combined with other elements or minerals in rocks. The rocks have to be processed to give pure metal. Rocks that contain metals that can be extracted are called mineral ORES. HEMATITE is an important ore from which we obtain iron. Much of our copper comes from a mineral called CHALCOPYRITE.

Mineral ores do not look like the metals that are made from

Metamorphic rocks are formed by heat and pressure, as when magma rises through the earth's crust or when rocks are folded to form new mountain ranges. Pressure and heat change limestone into marble, and pressure causes shale to change into the hard rock slate.

An iron ore mine: Iron, the most useful metal of the industrialized world, and already being mined some 5,000 years ago, is extracted from several mineral ores, including hematite and MAGNETITE.

them. They are not strong, hard, and shiny like most metals. Some are concentrated in layers of rock called VEINS. Sometimes they have been washed out of the solid rock and are found on the surface as grains of ore mixed with sand and gravel.

Mining

To obtain metals, mineral ores have to be removed from the ground and then treated in some way. Some ores are mined deep underground, but most are simply dug out of huge holes in the ground called quarries. Some

DIGGING DOWN

Boring into the earth's crust is difficult and expensive. In 1957 American scientists planned to drill through the thin oceanic crust and through the Moho to the mantle. The project was called the Mohole.

A test hole was drilled off the coast of Baja California. But in 1966, after millions of dollars had been spent, the U.S. Congress decided it could not spend any more money on the Mohole, and the idea was dropped.

The deepest mine in existence is 2.3 miles (3.78 km.) deep. It is a gold mine in South Africa.

The deepest hole bored into the crust is one the Russians are drilling in the Kola Peninsula, in northwest Russia, near the White Sea. The work began in 1970, and after 20 years the hole was more than 8 miles (13 km.) deep.

Geologists plan to carry on to 9 miles (15 km.). The temperature at the bottom of the hole is about twice that at which water boils.

quarries are 500 feet (150 meters) deep and cover several square miles.

Many ores are SMELTED, or melted, in order to remove impurities. Another process, called LEACHING, involves dissolving the metal from the ore and then recovering the metal from the liquid.

Aluminum comes from ores called BAUXITE. The bauxite is refined to produce a compound called alumina. The alumina is smelted to remove the oxygen in it and produce the metal. Pure aluminum is soft. To make it hard, it is mixed with small amounts of other metals. Mixtures of metals are called ALLOYS. Iron ore goes through similar processes. Iron is recovered from ores in blast furnaces and the iron is used to make steel alloys.

WEALTH FROM ROCKS

Building materials
Rock has been the most important building material from ancient times. Limestone, marble, and granite are used for many public buildings. Sand and clay are mixed to make bricks and tiles. Cement, made from powdered limestone and clay, is mixed with sand and water to make mortar. Add small stones and the mortar becomes concrete, the most common building material used today.

Metals and fuels
Copper, gold, and silver have always been highly prized but they are not as useful as iron, which with its alloy STEEL is used to make buildings, cars, aircraft, and weapons, and has hundreds of other industrial uses. So much high-grade iron has been mined that the world is now short of it.

The world is also running short of oil, which, like coal and gas, is found in layers in the rocks. As well as providing fuel, these

FOSSIL FUELS are used in the chemicals and plastics industries.

Even nuclear power comes from the rocks—from the RADIOACTIVE metal URANIUM.

MAKING COAL

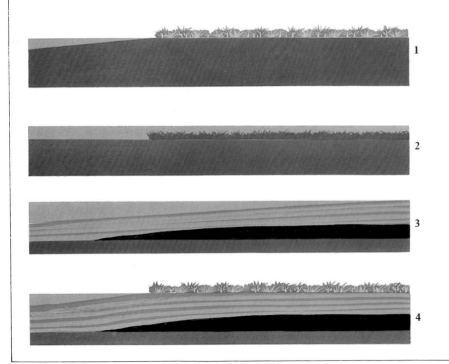

Coal is made up of the remains of plants that once grew in swampy forests. These ancient plants were submerged by water and compressed over millions of years. The more the material has been compressed, the harder it becomes and the hotter it burns. PEAT is soft, moist, and slow-burning. ANTHRACITE, the hardest coal, burns the hottest.

1 A swampy forest is flooded.
2 The trees die and mud and sand are deposited on them.
3 Under the weight, the trees turn to peat.
4 The sea level falls and the forest grows again on top of the hardened mud and sand. The peat hardens into coal.

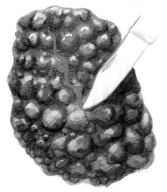

A penknife scraped across black hematite will leave a red mark.

TESTING MINERALS

Rocks are made of minerals, but the minerals are not always present in the same amounts. Separate pieces of the same kind of rock may be obviously different. For example, granite paving stones may be white, gray, pink, red, or black, depending on the mixture of minerals the rock contains.

Geologists identify minerals from several features, including their color, luster (shininess), hardness, specific gravity (their weight compared with an equal volume of water), crystal shape, transparency, the way they split, and so on.

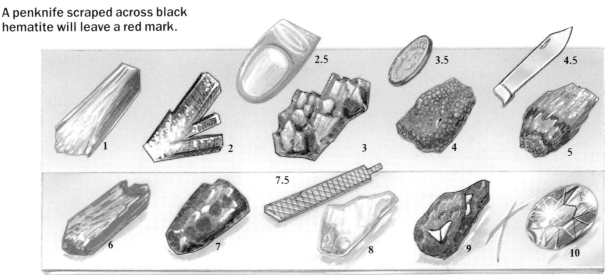

MOHS' SCALE

Each mineral has a certain hardness. Ten minerals are used to make up a table of hardness (named after a geologist, Friedrich Mohs) by which the hardness of other minerals can be measured. The softest is TALC (1) and the hardest diamond (10).

Other minerals or common objects can be used to test for hardness. For example, calcite (3) scratches gypsum (2) but will not scratch FLUORITE (4). A fingernail has a hardness of 2.5. It will scratch gypsum but not calcite. A steel file will scratch quartz (7) but not TOPAZ (8). Softer minerals (1–5) can be scratched by glass, while harder ones (6–10) will scratch glass.

Crystals form when molten rock cools and becomes solid. Crystals are often very beautiful and some, such as emeralds, are highly prized.

Drifting Continents

In the past 40 years, astonishing discoveries have been made about the oceans. Using special techniques, geologists have studied earth's crust under the sea bed. Much of the ocean floor has been mapped with instruments called echo sounders. A drilling ship called the *Glomar Challenger* has roamed the oceans, drilling into the floor of the ABYSS, the deep ocean, to take samples of the rocks underneath.

The most important discovery was further proof that the continents are moving about. The idea of continental drift, as it is called, was first put forward in 1912 by a German scientist, Alfred Wegener.

If you look at a map of the South Atlantic Ocean, you will see that the bulge of South America looks as though it ought to fit into Africa, like pieces in a jigsaw puzzle. Wegener suggested that it must have done so long ago.

He noticed that if you fitted the two continents together, mountain ranges of the same age and type would be next to each other. Wegener also discovered that areas of South America, Africa, and Australia had once been covered by ice. Had they once been at the South Pole? Wegener thought they must have been, but other people scoffed.

Evidence ignored

There was some more evidence that convinced Wegener that he was right. Scientists know that different kinds of animals have evolved in different parts of the world. For example, animals in Australia are not like those in Europe or Africa. Yet the fossils of certain animals were found in different continents, landmasses

On an ordinary map the edges of the landmasses look as if they might fit together. On a computer map of the CONTINENTAL SHELVES (pale blue), which are the true edges of the continents, the fit is almost perfect.

long separated by wide oceans. How did they get there unless the continents were linked?

Wegener was certain that the continents must once have been joined together, but the scientific community of the day was not impressed. Since Wegener was neither a qualified geologist nor PALEONTOLOGIST (student of fossils), nobody took him seriously. How could continents move? What force could thrust landmasses so far apart? Wegener was a METEOROLOGIST. He should stick to predicting the weather.

The weather, however, was another part of the puzzle of the continents. The fossilized remains of tropical forests are found in places that now have very cold climates. There is evidence that the area that is now the Sahara Desert in Africa was once covered with ice. Had the

EVIDENCE OF DRIFT

About 200 million years ago, all the present-day continents were joined together in one huge landmass called Pangaea, the southern part of which was at one time situated at the South Pole. In due course Pangaea split up into several continents. Scientists have discovered a variety of evidence to prove this.

Magnetized particles contained in old rocks show that the single continent gradually moved over the South Pole between 300 and 200 million years ago.

Geologists have also discovered evidence of glaciation—sheets of ice covering the land—in Africa as far north as the Sahara, which is now desert.

Rocks on the west coast of Africa and the east coast of South America have been found to be exactly alike, providing evidence that the two continents were once joined.

Further proof comes from the discovery of identical fossils of animals and plants in different continents. These could not have evolved on separate landmasses or reached them by sea. They include a land reptile called *Lystrosaurus*, a freshwater reptile called *Mesosaurus*, and plants called *Glossopteris*.

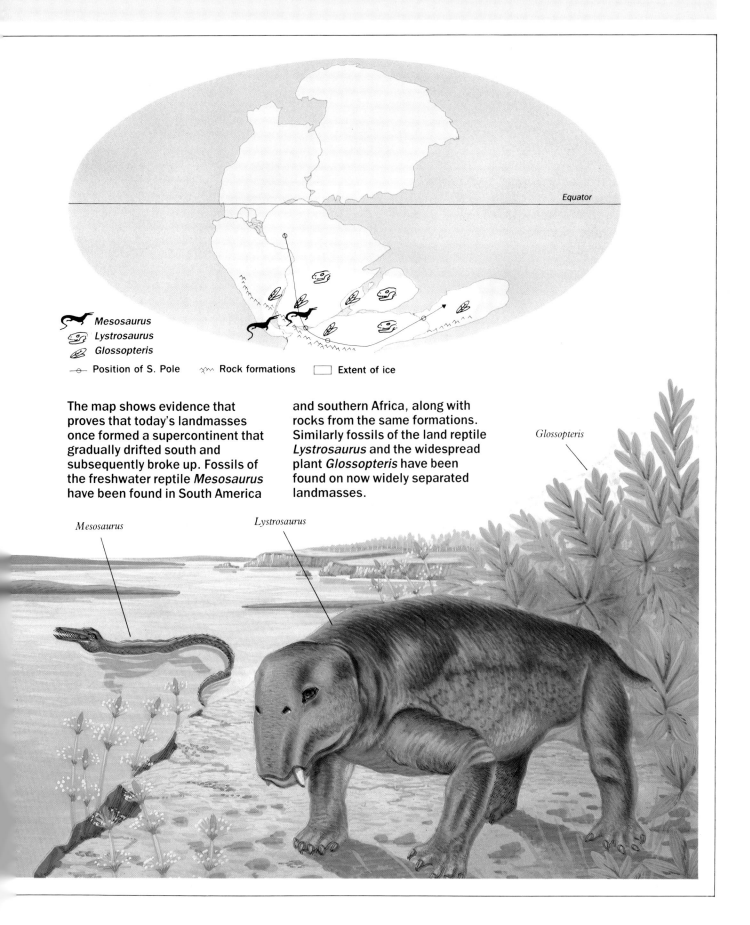

Mesosaurus
Lystrosaurus
Glossopteris
Position of S. Pole   Rock formations   Extent of ice

The map shows evidence that proves that today's landmasses once formed a supercontinent that gradually drifted south and subsequently broke up. Fossils of the freshwater reptile *Mesosaurus* have been found in South America and southern Africa, along with rocks from the same formations. Similarly fossils of the land reptile *Lystrosaurus* and the widespread plant *Glossopteris* have been found on now widely separated landmasses.

Equator

Glossopteris

Mesosaurus

Lystrosaurus

climate in those parts of the world drastically changed, or had the continents changed position?

Secrets of the ocean

The evidence for Wegener's theory lay under the sea. When the oceans were mapped in the 1950s and 1960s, scientists discovered long undersea mountain ranges called OCEAN RIDGES. Along the entire length of the ridges ran deep RIFT VALLEYS. Volcanoes, many hidden from view, were scattered alongside the mountains. In places, the volcanoes surfaced as islands. Elsewhere there were long, deep OCEAN TRENCHES, some of them more than 6 miles (10 kilometers) below sea level.

The scientists worked out the age of the undersea rocks and found that the rocks in the rift valleys were newer than those beside them. Another discovery was that the ridges were unstable. Not only did their volcanoes erupt continually, but there were also frequent earthquakes. There were earthquakes along the deep ocean trenches, too. Surely the rocks must be moving to provoke such activity?

Magnetic proof

The final proof came from the earth's magnetism. Nearly all

The ocean ridges are the world's longest mountain ranges. The rift valleys running down the centers of the ridges are composed of young rocks with hotter temperatures than the rocks on either side. This means that new crustal rock is continually being formed along the slopes of these underwater valleys.

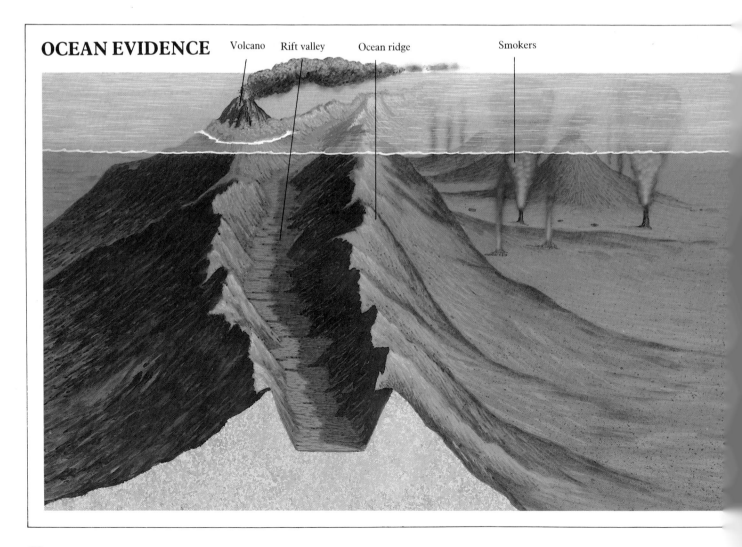

OCEAN EVIDENCE Volcano Rift valley Ocean ridge Smokers

rocks contain tiny quantities of iron, a metal that can be magnetized by other magnets. The particles of iron in these rocks were slightly magnetized by earth's own magnetism when they were laid down millions of years ago.

Every magnet has two poles. If you have two magnets, you can see that opposite poles attract each other and same poles repel. Each iron particle in the rock had a north and south pole. The south pole pointed to the earth's North Pole and the north to the South. As the hot rocks cooled, the magnetism became fixed. The material of a kiln, or any place where things are baked to a high temperature, becomes magnetized in the same way.

In the 1960s delicate instruments called magnetometers were towed over the seabed to measure the strength of the magnetism of the ocean floor. Some strange variations were found.

It has now been proved that earth's polarity reverses from time to time—that is, the north and south magnetic poles change places. The switchover has happened about 20 times in the past five million years. These changes of polarity have left a series of magnetic "stripes" in the ocean

Alongside the deep ocean trenches, where earthquakes are common, are chains of volcanic islands. And in places along ocean ridges, superheated water gushes from deep clefts in the ocean floor. The water is colored by minerals from the newly formed rock. These boiling springs are called SMOKERS.

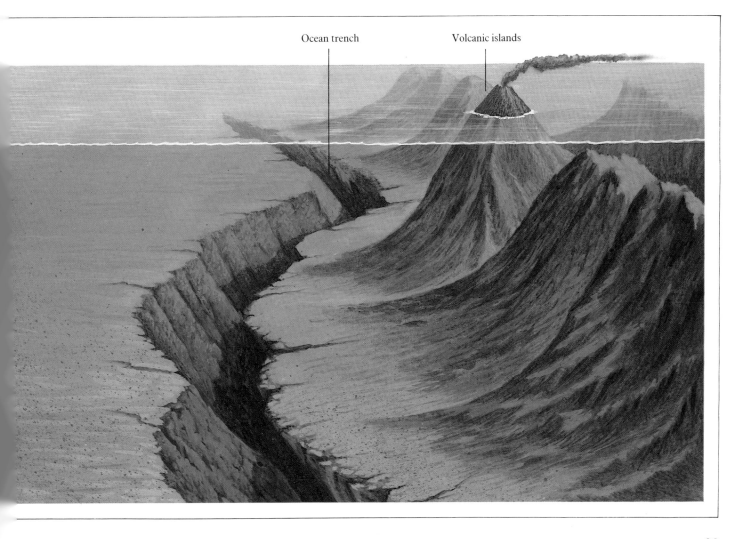
Ocean trench   Volcanic islands

floor, on either side of the mid-ocean ridges. They proved beyond doubt that the ages of the rocks varied.

The scientists found that the rocks in the rift valleys of the ridges were the youngest in the oceans. Away from the ridges on both sides, the rocks were older and older. No rocks on the ocean floor are more than 200 million years old. By contrast, rocks on the continents range in age from a few million to more than 3 billion years.

Moving plates

From all these clues, scientists came up with a new theory called PLATE TECTONICS. Earth's crust is not a continuous unbroken layer, like the shell of an egg. It is split into large, rigid blocks called plates. The plates are moved around by currents in the molten

HOT CURRENTS

If you put a pan of water on the stove (left), the water nearest the heat becomes hot and rises. Cooler water from the top sinks to take its place. Then it, too, rises, and so on. As the water gets hotter, it continues to circulate in currents in the saucepan. Molten rock in the upper mantle behaves in the same way. The currents in the magma cause the land above to move.

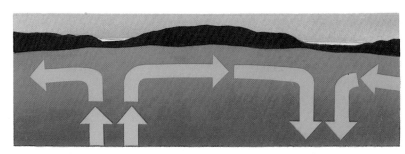

RESTLESS CRUST

Fold mountains
(plates collide)

Oceanic ridge
(plates move apart)

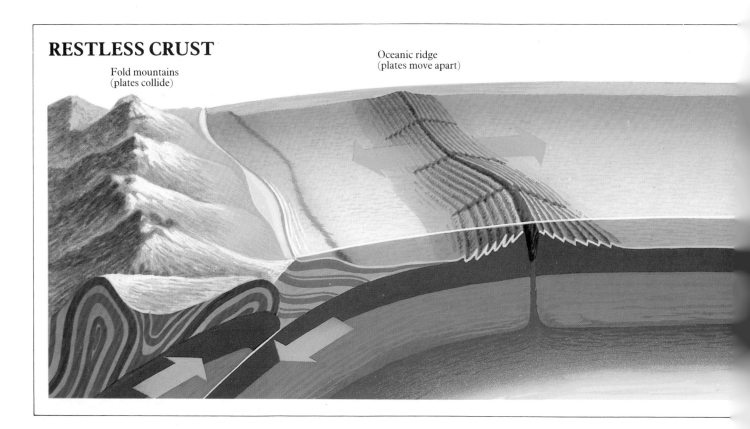

rock in the upper mantle. The rift valleys in the center of the midocean ridges are the edges of plates. Here new crustal rocks are continually being formed as two plates move apart.

Destroying plates

As new material is being added to plates in one place, old material is being destroyed in another. The deep ocean trenches are the sites of destruction. There the edges of the plates meet, and one plate is sucked beneath another into the interior of earth. The edge of the descending plate grows hot and melts, creating magma. Some of this magma rises up to reach the surface, forming volcanoes.

Chains of volcanic islands have been formed in this way. On land, volcanoes occur along a line close to a deep ocean trench. An example of this is the chain of volcanoes in the Andes Mountains of South America. There is an ocean trench near the western coast of that continent.

Plates do not generally slip gently under each other. Some collide with great force, slowly crumpling the land into mountains or provoking violent earthquakes that cause great cracks and fissures in the land and overturn the rocks.

The changing continents

The theory of plate tectonics is now accepted by almost all geologists. It explains how, why, and where earthquakes and volcanoes occur, how the continents once fitted together, how the remains of sea creatures can be found at the tops of mountains, and why icy continents bear evidence of periods of baking heat.

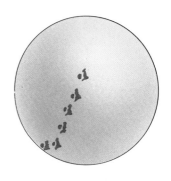

The British Isles are part of the continent of Europe. They have drifted—with the continent—5,600 miles (9,000 kilometers) in the last 500 million years.

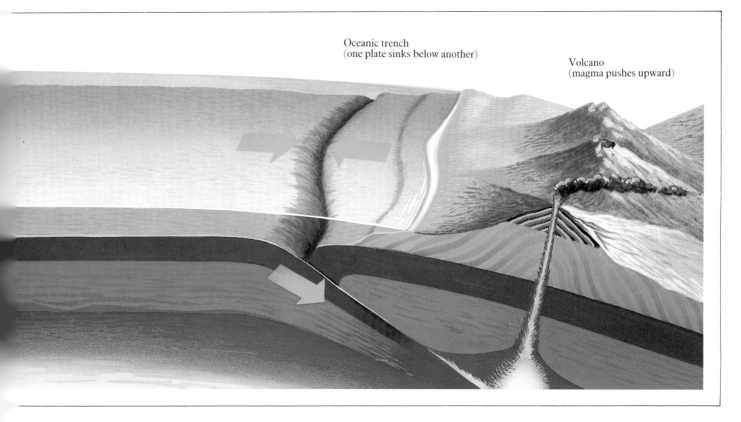

Oceanic trench
(one plate sinks below another)

Volcano
(magma pushes upward)

Changing places

About 420 million years ago, there were four landmasses. One, called Gondwanaland, consisted of all the present-day southern continents. Two of the others (present-day Europe and North America) collided, throwing up the Appalachian Mountains in North America and mountains in Greenland, Scandinavia, and the British Isles. The new continent then collided with Asia, and the Urals were formed.

About 200 million years ago all the present continents were joined together in one huge landmass. Scientists call this supercontinent Pangaea. Around 140 million years ago, Pangaea broke into two smaller supercontinents. The northern one, known as Laurasia, contained present-day North America, Europe, and most of Asia. The southern one, called Gondwanaland, contained the rest, including India.

When Laurasia broke up, the Atlantic Ocean was formed. The ocean began as a small gap about 40 million years ago. The Atlantic is still growing wider, at the rate of about 1 inch every year, as America moves away from Europe. Another movement that has been measured is in the Red Sea. Arabia is swinging away from Africa, to which it was once joined.

Continents today

There are seven continents today. In descending order of size, they are Asia, Africa, North America, South America, Antarctica, Europe, and Australia. The continents are huge, unbroken land areas surrounded, or largely surrounded, by water. They also include nearby islands,

JIGSAW EARTH

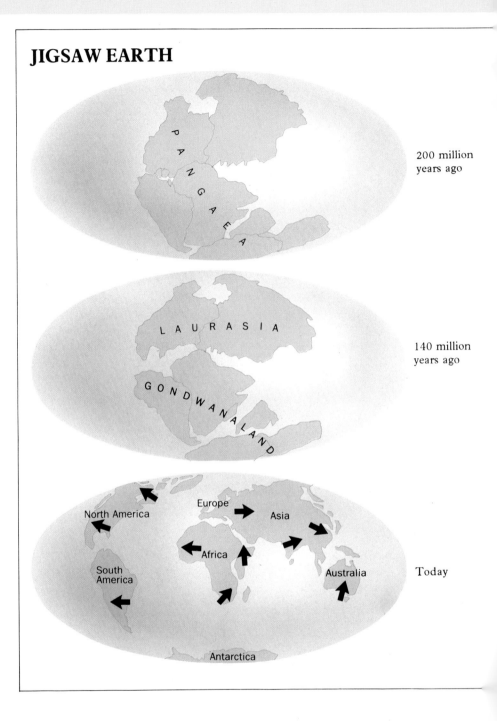

200 million years ago

140 million years ago

Today

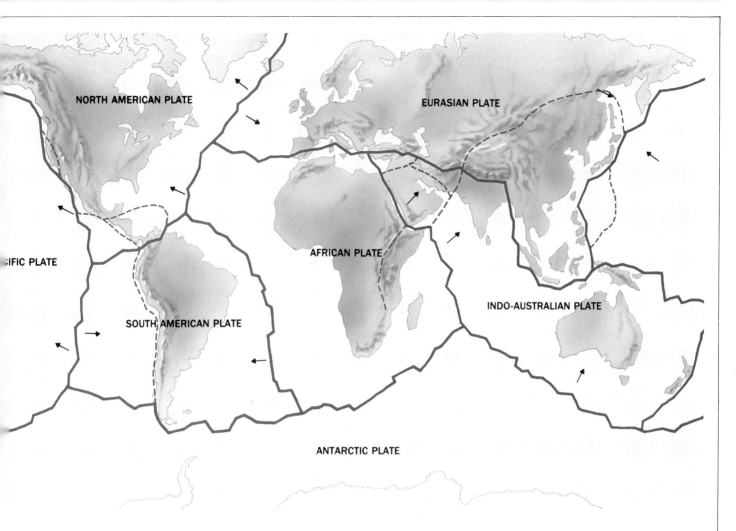

The maps (left) show how the continents have moved during the last 200 million years. The supercontinent of Pangaea split up into two smaller ones, Laurasia and Gondwanaland. Gradually the continents moved to their present positions (above).

The earth's hard outer shell is split into seven enormous plates and several smaller ones. Plate movements have been going on throughout most of the earth's history and are continuing to this day. The arrows indicate the direction of their movement. If the plates continue to move as they are, the Atlantic Ocean will be far wider in 50 million years' time than it is today, and Australia will be farther north, pushing up against the continent of Asia.

which lie on the continental shelves. Examples are Great Britain and Ireland, off the coast of continental Europe, Madagascar off the coast of Africa, and Sri Lanka off the coast of India in Asia.

Europe and Asia have a long land border, which runs along the Ural Mountains and the Ural River, and then through the Caspian Sea and the Caucasus Mountains. Because of this long border, Europe and Asia are sometimes considered to be one giant continent, called Eurasia. The two continents joined up many millions of years ago.

Africa is joined to Asia along the line of the Suez Canal, while North and South America are linked by a thin strip of land, the Isthmus of Panama. Antarctica and Australia are surrounded by water. Australia is the only continent that is also a country. Australia, New Zealand, and Papua New Guinea are often called Australasia or Oceania. Antarctica is covered with ice.

Earthquakes and Volcanoes

In January 1980 there was an enormous explosion in the state of Washington in the north-western United States. Mount Saint Helens had erupted. A plug of solid lava was blown out of the top of the mountain, and a huge cloud of dust and ash rose into the sky. Since then, Mount Saint Helens has erupted many times, though less dramatically.

In 1988, in Armenia, a violent shock wave caused an earthquake that killed 25,000 people and made many more homeless. Both events were caused by movements in the earth's crust, as tectonic plates edged against each other.

Waking and sleeping

Volcanoes are holes in the surface of the earth, through which gas, steam, and molten rock erupt. All around the world volcanoes are erupting all the time, some gently, some violently. Others are dormant, quietly sleeping until they rumble awake, like Mount Saint Helens, which had not erupted since 1857. Others sleep forever. Edinburgh Castle in Scotland sits atop the cold hard rock of an extinct volcano.

Mount Saint Helens lies near the edge of a plate that is being pushed under the North American landmass. Most active volcanoes occur on or near plate margins and result from the movement of plates against each other. Extinct volcanoes like the one in Edinburgh are on old plate margins that are now fused solid.

The shaking earth

Countless earthquakes occur every year, but most are so slight that the waves caused by their vibrating movements are

CRACKS IN THE OCEAN FLOOR

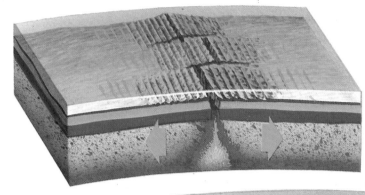

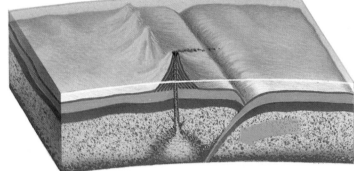

Through the center of the long ocean ridges are deep cracks where new rock is being formed (top). Elsewhere the edges of plates are being destroyed as they plunge into deep trenches. All this activity causes earthquakes and volcanoes.

detected only by sensitive instruments called SEISMOGRAPHS. Most earthquakes occur when rocks move along FAULTS, or cracks, in the earth's crust. Plates do not move smoothly. Their edges are jagged and they become locked together. Gradually strain builds up as currents of molten rock inside the earth push and pull at the overlying plates. Eventually the strain becomes so great that the plates lurch in a sudden movement, causing the ground to shake. The seismograph pinpoints the area where the earthquake has occurred and measures its strength but gives no advance warning of a quake.

Ring of Fire

Earthquakes and volcanoes can occur anywhere, but the most severe occur near plate edges. If you look at a map on which earthquakes and volcanoes are plotted, you will see two great belts. One follows the edge of the Pacific Ocean and is called the Pacific Ring of Fire. The other crosses southern Europe, northern Africa, and parts of Asia.

Earthquake and active volcano zones follow the ocean ridges and ocean trenches. Most earth-

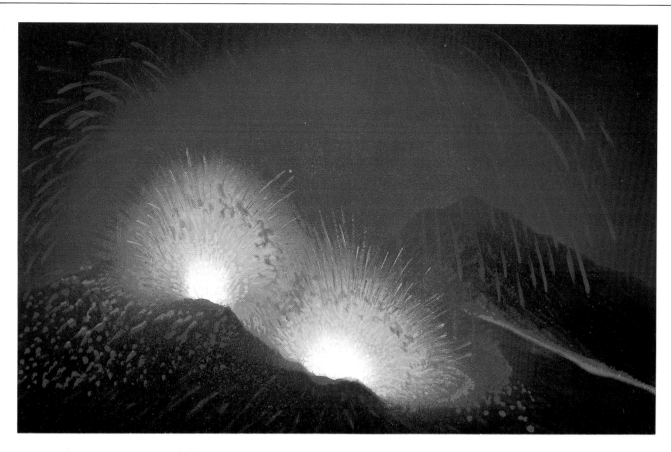

TYPES OF VOLCANO

Active erupts all the time (Mount Stromboli, Italy)

Intermittent erupts from time to time (Mount Etna, Italy)

Dormant has not erupted for a long time (Mount Fuji, Japan)

Extinct has not erupted within recorded history (Mount Kilimanjaro, Tanzania).

RING OF FIRE

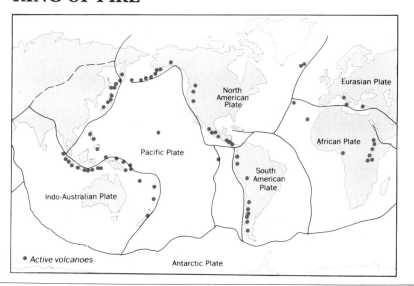

• Active volcanoes

quakes occur under the sea and do little harm, except when they set off TIDAL WAVES called TSUNA-MIS. Those that occur in inhabited land areas often cause great damage and loss of life.

There are more than 500 active volcanoes on dry land. About three-quarters of these lie around the Pacific. Some lie near ocean trenches where descending plates are melted. Others lie along ocean ridges where plates are moving apart. A few lie far from plate edges. The molten material in these volcanoes is probably produced by HOT SPOTS, isolated sources of heat in the mantle.

They include the volcanoes of the Hawaiian Islands in the Pacific.

Death and destruction

The most severe earthquakes often occur along TRANSFORM FAULTS, where two plates are sliding past each other. Sometimes they cause only a series of small quakes, but when plates move suddenly, the effects can be devastating. One of the most severe quakes occurred along the San Andreas Fault in California in 1906. A sudden movement, of about 19 feet (6 meters), caused enormous damage in San Francisco and several nearby towns. About 700 people died. In the center of San Francisco huge fires broke out, causing millions of dollars' worth of damage. The San Andreas Fault moved again in 1989. It was a much smaller movement. Even so it caused 62 deaths, destroyed buildings, wrecked a major bridge and highway, and set off fires.

The 1906 earthquake is by no means the worst in modern times. The Tangshan earthquake in eastern China in 1976 caused between 242,000 and 750,000 deaths (there is some dispute about the numbers). The worst recorded earthquake death toll occurred in the lands around the eastern end of the Mediterranean in 1201. Deaths were estimated at 1,100,000.

CALIFORNIA QUAKE

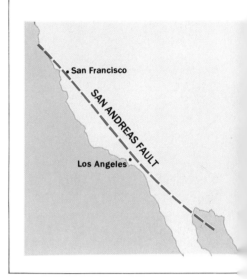

NEW VOLCANOES

A farmer in the Mexican village of Paricutín was plowing a field one day in 1943 when he saw a plume of smoke coming out of the ground. It was the start of a volcano. Within a week it had grown into a CINDER CONE 492 feet (150 meters) high. Mount Paricutín is now 7,451 feet (2,271 meters) high.

In 1963 a plume of smoke rose from the sea off Iceland. It was another underwater volcano. Within weeks it had grown into an island, now named Surtsey. Iceland straddles the Mid-Atlantic Ridge, and is full of volcanoes and GEYSERS. Surtsey gave scientists a chance to study how quickly the new island became colonized with plant and animal life once it had cooled down.

VIOLENT AND GENTLE VOLCANOES

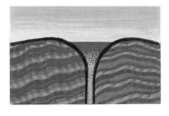

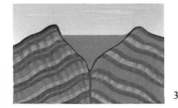

Volcanic eruptions can be gentle or violent. Some volcanoes suddenly explode, flinging out rocks and lava in a furious burst. From others lava seeps gently and spreads over the land.

1 In a typical explosive volcano, pressure from fiery gas-filled magma builds up until it explodes with massive force, hurling rocks, steam, ash, and large lumps of molten lava into the air. In time, a tall cone builds up around the vent with a crater at the top.
2 A SHIELD VOLCANO builds up a flatter mound as runny lava gently spills out of it.
3 Between eruptions, volcanoes are dormant (sleeping). Volcanoes where all activity has ceased are extinct. Sometimes their craters fill with water to form lakes called CALDERAS.

The San Andreas Fault is a transform fault that runs up the California coast. A severe quake, like the one of 1906, may occur at any time.

Anatomy of a volcano

The magma under the earth's crust contains a high proportion of gas and water, held at high pressure. When the pressure becomes very high, it forces a crack in the crust. The gas escapes through this VENT and the magma becomes lava. If the lava flows readily, the gas escapes easily and the eruption is said to be "quiet." If the lava is very thick, the trapped gas explodes, producing an eruption of lava, lumps of rock (called volcanic bombs), dust, and ash.

Thin lava spreads over a wide area around the vent through which it emerges. Successive lava flows build up into a gently sloping dome, like an upturned saucer. Such volcanoes are called shield volcanoes. Iceland and the Hawaiian Islands have large shield volcanoes.

When only ash and rocks are hurled from the vent of the volcano, they build up into an ash or cinder cone. Mount Paricutín in Mexico is a typical cinder cone.

Mount Fuji in Japan and Mount Egmont in New Zealand are typical intermediate or COMPOSITE VOLCANOES. These huge cone-shaped mountains are made of alternate layers of volcanic ash and other fragments from explosive eruptions and lava from quiet eruptions.

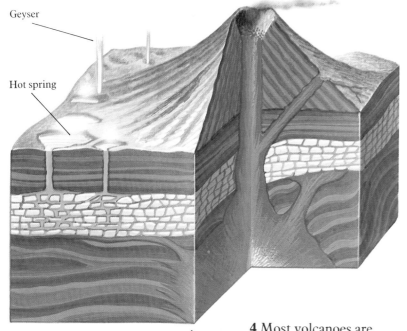

Geyser

Hot spring

4

4 Most volcanoes are intermediate. They may erupt explosively or quietly, and build up slopes of ash and lava. Lava may spill from vents in the sides, and nearby there may be geysers and hot springs with water heated by the magma below ground.

RICHTER SCALE

SEISMOLOGISTS, people who study earthquakes, use a scale to indicate the strength of each earthquake. It is named after Charles F. Richter, the American who devised it. Each number on the scale indicates an earthquake ten times as strong as the number below. So far the strongest earthquakes have not exceeded 8.9 on the scale.

There are many "listening stations" around the world, which detect about 500,000 earthquakes every year. Only about 100,000 of them can be felt, and of these only about 1,000 are severe enough to cause damage to property. After every big earthquake there are a number of aftershocks, some of them fairly violent, as the ground settles down again.

Mountains

A mountain is an area of the earth's surface that rises considerably above the surrounding land. It often has steep, rocky sides that are difficult to climb. Many mountains form part of much larger areas of high ground. A group or line of mountains is called a mountain range, or mountain chain.

Mountains cover more than a quarter of the earth's surface. This figure includes mountains under the sea, of which there are many. The midocean ridges are mountain chains. The peaks of some undersea mountains emerge from the sea as islands. They include the islands of the West Indies and the scattered islands of the Pacific Ocean.

Some mountain ranges include areas of fairly level land, almost as high as the mountaintops. These lofty plains are called PLATEAUS. Most of Tibet is a plateau, the highest in the world.

The greatest mountain range in the world is the Himalayas. It separates the Indian sub-

FOLD MOUNTAINS

Mount Everest is the world's highest mountain. It is one of 109 peaks that rise more than 24,000 feet (7,300 meters) high, 96 of which are in the Himalaya and Karakoram ranges in central Asia. Their peaks are snow-covered year-round because they are so high. All of them are typical fold mountains.

Rocks deep in the earth are hot and can be melted or bent like slabs of warm toffee (opposite). Instead of bending, some of these rocks tend to break as they fold, crumbling up into mountains as plates collide. Simple folds are SYNCLINES and ANTICLINES. An ANTICLINORIUM is a collection of anticlines. Some folds turn on their sides. These are called RECUMBENT FOLDS. Sometimes

folds are snapped and are pushed up over other rocks. These are called NAPPES.

Often you cannot see the original shape of a fold mountain because its surface rocks have been worn away by erosion, which gradually reduces the height and jaggedness of any mountain.

continent from the rest of Asia. The highest mountain is Mount Everest, on the border between Nepal and Tibet. Other huge mountain chains are in the Americas, notably the Rocky Mountains of North America and the Andes of South America, and in Europe, notably the Alps and the Caucasus Mountains.

MOUNTAIN HEIGHTS

The height of a mountain is always worked out as the height of its peak above mean (average) SEA LEVEL, even though the mountain may be a long way from the ocean. It is never given as the height above the surrounding land. To be called a mountain, the land must generally be more than 2,300 feet (700 meters) above sea level. High ground lower than that is called a hill.

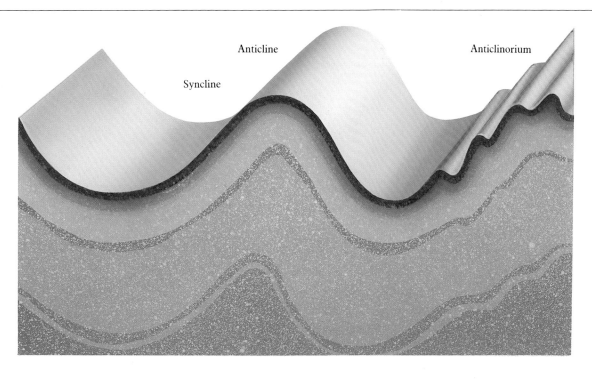

Syncline · Anticline · Anticlinorium

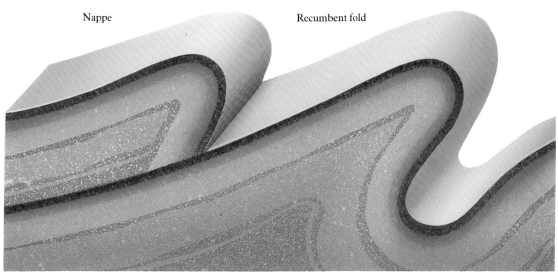

Nappe · Recumbent fold

Kinds of mountains

There are three types of mountains: volcanoes, fold mountains, and BLOCK MOUNTAINS. The world's greatest mountain ranges, the Himalayas, Rockies, Andes, and Alps, are all fold mountains. These ranges were all formed as a result of one plate colliding with another and causing enormous pressure on the rocks.

Originally the ground was flat. The rocks were sedimentary, formed from sediments such as sand and clay that had been laid down in layers on the seabed. The pressure of the collision between the plates caused the rocks to bend and twist, rise up to great heights, and tower over the older continental masses on either side. The ocean gave place to land.

Movement of these colliding plates is still going on. It is thought that the Himalayas are slowly growing higher. There is a great deal of unrest along the Andes, shown by the active volcanoes and frequent earthquakes in the region.

Types of folds

Folds occur in many shapes and sizes. Some are mere crinkles, a few feet long. Others may be huge. A downward fold, like a trough, is called a syncline; an upward fold, like an arch, is called an anticline. A fold lying on its side is a recumbent fold. Sometimes a recumbent fold breaks off, so that the upper half is pushed sideways over the lower half. A fold like this is called a nappe.

Sometimes the original layers of rock are so folded that the layers are vertical or even upside down. Fossils embedded in the rocks help experts decide the correct order in which the rocks were laid down.

Land at fault

Sometimes when two plates meet head-on or scrape against each other, the rocks between them do not fold, but break. Breaks, or fractures, also occur if two parts of a plate are pulled apart. Breaks in rock layers are called faults.

Faults usually occur in groups, and some extend for thousands of feet down into the earth's crust. The rocks on either side of the fault move, sometimes downward, sometimes upward, and sometimes sideways. The San Andreas Fault is an example of one block of land moving sideways against another.

If two deep faults occur roughly parallel to each other, the block of land between may be heaved up to form a block mountain. The Ruwenzori Mountains on the equator in central Africa are 50 miles (80 kilometers) across and over 16,400 feet (5,000 meters) high. They are an example of a huge block of crust uplifted between faults. The mountains are 40 miles (65 kilometers) across and about 75 miles (120 kilometers) long. The highest peaks are more than 16,400 feet (5,000 meters) above sea level.

Some block mountains have flat tops and form high plateaus. Others, such as the Black Forest and Vosges Mountains in Europe, form long ridges.

A block of land between two faults may drop down to form a steep-sided rift valley. The biggest rift valley in the world is the Great Rift Valley in Africa.

The main tools of erosion are running water, heat, frost, ice, and—in dry areas—wind. Most erosion takes place slowly, but occasionally landslides and rockfalls achieve as much in a few minutes as the other kinds of erosion achieve in a thousand years.

Dome mountains

Only a little of the magma that rises from the mantle into the earth's crust reaches the surface. Most of it forces its way between layers of rock in the crust and becomes trapped there. Eventually it cools and sets into hard intrusive rock, such as granite.

Rocks formed in this way may be in thin horizontal sheets (sills) or in huge masses (batholiths) many feet wide and deep. When huge bodies of magma rise vertically through the crust, they may push the overlying rock layers into great dome mountains.

Rocks formed underground are usually tougher and harder than the rocks above and around them. We can see granite rocks formed from molten magma in many places where the overlying, softer rocks have been worn away. The Sierra Nevada range in California and the Cairngorm Mountains in Scotland are made of intrusive rocks that have been exposed on the surface.

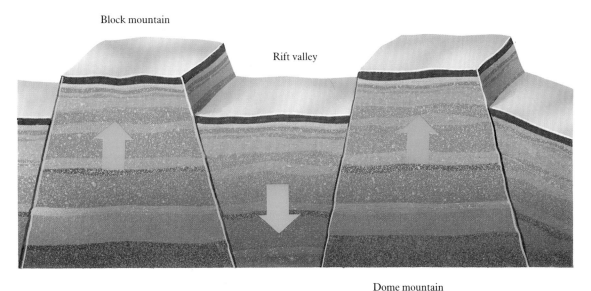

Block mountain

Rift valley

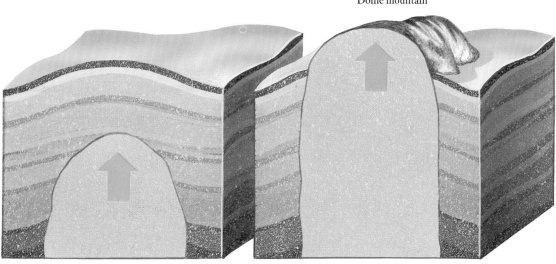

Dome mountain

Erosion

The surface of the earth is constantly being worn away by the effects of changing temperatures and the action of wind, running water, waves, and ice. This process is called erosion. Slowly but surely, even the hardest rocks are reduced to pebbles and sand. Over millions of years great mountain ranges are created and slowly worn flat. Even the mighty Himalayas will eventually be smoothed away by erosion.

Weathering

One kind of erosion is called weathering. In hot climates, especially deserts, rocks may be heated during the day and get very cold at night. When rocks get hot they expand; when they cool they contract. Repeated expanding and contracting weakens the rock and pieces flake off.

In cool, rainy places, such as mountains, water seeps into cracks in rocks and freezes into ice. When water turns to ice, it increases in size by about a tenth. As it freezes, the expanding ice pushes against the sides of the cracks and forces them apart. After this has happened many times, the rocks may shatter or be split in two.

Pieces of rock that have broken off slide down the mountainside. Gradually they pile up into sloping banks of stones and boulders called SCREE.

WATER VAPOR absorbs CARBON DIOXIDE from the air, which makes it slightly acidic. Though it is only a weak solution, the acid is strong enough to eat away limestone rock. Mountains made of limestone are worn down in this way.

Limestone is full of horizontal joints, called bedding planes, and

DESERT WEATHERING

The ground of the desert is baking hot by day. At night the temperature drops dramatically and the ground shrinks, causing it to crack. Rock surfaces, too, are very hot by day and cold at night. Surface shrinking causes whole layers to peel off.

Wind and weather carve strange shapes by eating away at the rock nearest the ground. The softer the rock, the more quickly it is worn away.

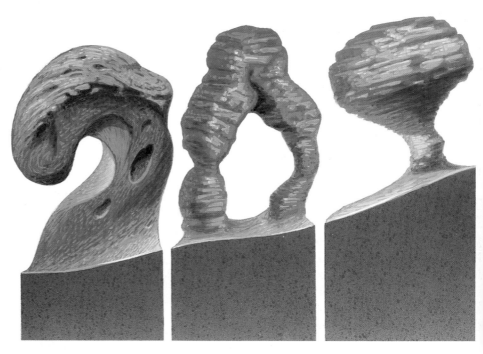

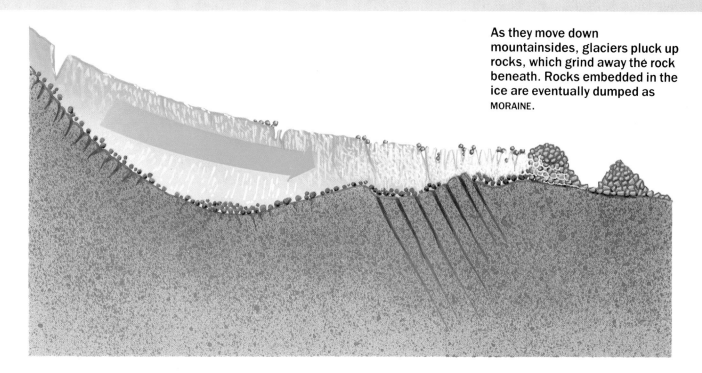

As they move down mountainsides, glaciers pluck up rocks, which grind away the rock beneath. Rocks embedded in the ice are eventually dumped as MORAINE.

vertical cracks. Acid water seeps into these cracks and washes out the rock, very slowly. This is why limestone mountains often have caves in them, and the caves sometimes have rivers running through them.

Even in deserts, water weathers the rocks. Surface cracks may open up when rocks get hot, and this allows water from occasional rainstorms or dew to get into them. The water often has salt dissolved in it. When the water dries up in the hot sun, the salt is left behind. Over many years a layer of salt crystals builds up, and the rock surface is forced apart. Eventually the surface flakes off.

The wind at work
In dry regions winds pick up particles of dust and sand and hurl them at the rocks. Little by little the particles wear away the rocks like a natural sandblaster. Because the particles are heavy, the wind cannot lift them high

SHAPED BY ICE

Many features of mountain scenery result from the work of ice. Steep-sided basins, called CIRQUES, show where a glacier originated at the head of a broad-bottomed, steep-sided valley. Knife-edged ridges, called ARÊTES, separate neighboring cirques. Tall waterfalls pour down the valley sides, while lakes lie in hollows scraped out by ice.

off the ground, so most wind erosion takes place at ground level. The rocks higher up are untouched. With their bases eroded and their tops not, the rocks look top-heavy. They are called mushroom rocks. Softer rock is eroded more quickly than harder rock, which results in even stranger shapes.

Ice in action

High up a mountain the air is so cold that most of the moisture that falls there is snow. Below a certain level, the snow melts in summer, but all the higher parts remain snow-clad. The lower limit of this perpetual snow is called the SNOW LINE.

Above the snow line the snow piles up, year after year. The fresh snow weighs down on the snow beneath it. After years of pressure the bottom layer of snow becomes compacted into ice. As the ice layer grows thicker, it becomes heavier, and it slips gradually downhill under its own weight. The snow has become a glacier, a river of ice.

Valleys

Like rivers, glaciers form valleys as they move downhill. You can tell a valley that has been carved by a glacier by its U-shaped bottom. A river valley is more like a V. Rocks embedded in the ice scrape away at the rock underneath, scouring and smoothing it.

As the temperature rises further down the mountain, the glacier begins to melt. The rocks embedded in the ice are dumped. Mounds of frost-shattered clay and rock, called moraine, lie discarded by the melting ice at the end of the glacier.

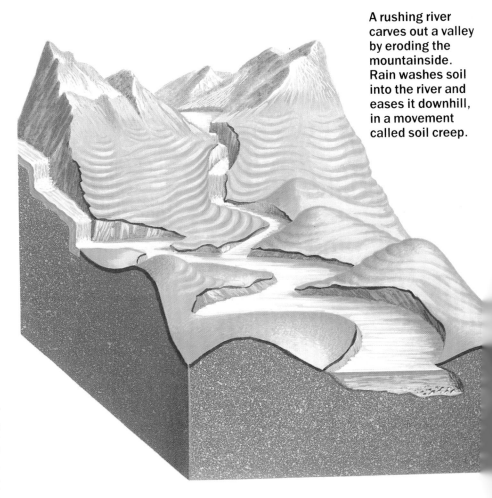

A rushing river carves out a valley by eroding the mountainside. Rain washes soil into the river and eases it downhill, in a movement called soil creep.

Rivers and rainfall

The greatest effect on the landscape is made by rivers. Rivers flowing swiftly downhill pick up and deposit fragments of rock that scour out steep-sided valleys. The faster the flow, the more severe the erosion and the deeper the valleys. As the rivers widen and flood, more and more rock and sediment are carried along. Eventually the rivers deposit huge loads of sediment into the sea.

The erosive work of the rivers is aided by rain. Raindrops batter valley sides, like billions of sharp chisels. They loosen splinters of rock and splash fine grains of soil into the air.

The work of the sea

On the coast, waves carrying sand and pebbles pound the shore. They cut into the rock face and weaken its base. Eventually the rock, soil, and vegetation above collapse, leaving a bare cliff. Sometimes the action of the waves on soft rock cuts caves in the cliffs. On some headlands the waves, pounding both sides, gradually cause two caves to join up and the rock above forms an arch.

Deposition

Sooner or later all the rock that is worn from one place is deposited in another. A river dumps part of its load of sediment on its FLOOD-

THE DUST BOWL

The Great Plains of the United States were originally covered by grass, which holds soil together in a way that wheat, which is replanted each year, does not. Too much plowing and exposure of the topsoil weakened the soil's staying power. A period of severe DROUGHT, which began in 1931, was accompanied in 1934–1935 by violent and destructive winds. The storms resulted in a devastating series of dust storms in an area on the borders of Kansas, Colorado, New Mexico, Texas, and Oklahoma. The soil just blew away, and spread over states to the east. It left large areas of the Great Plains ruined. The drought ended in 1938, but by then the damage had been done. The area has been further damaged by dust storms several times since.

ACID RAIN

Whenever we burn oil, coal, or gas, chemical compounds are released into the atmosphere. These react with water vapor in the air to form acids. These acids fall to the ground by themselves or in rain. Nobody knows how much harm they do, but in many ancient cities you can see the damage that has been done to old buildings. Some that have withstood wind and rain for pollution-free centuries are now black and crumbling. Lakes and rivers become too acidic for fish and other wildlife to survive. Soil becomes too acid for crops to grow well, and vast areas of forest are blighted by acid from nearby industries. Every time you ride a bike instead of a bus or car, you may be helping to save the environment.

PLAIN, the rest on the shore or in the sea. In some places, instead of wearing away rocks, the sea carries sand, pebbles, and gravel from one place and dumps it in another, where a new beach or a SPIT of land is formed. A glacier sheds its moraine. Desert winds sweep the sand into huge moving seas of DUNES.

Heavy rain on steep slopes sometimes causes landslides. The soil becomes saturated and some of it "floats" on the rainwater. On a steep slope, there may be nothing to hold the soil back and large slabs of it slither downward, smashing everything in its path. Trees growing naturally or planted on hillsides help to prevent floods and AVALANCHES. Their roots bind the soil and help it soak up water. Their foliage acts as an umbrella over the soil.

Human erosion

Natural erosion is slow and inevitable. Erosion caused by people is often speedy, unnecessary, and catastrophic. When forests are cut down and grasslands are plowed, the soil is exposed to wind and rain. Tree roots bind the soil; without them landslips and floods occur. Wind can strip the topsoil from fields and intensive farming can rob the soil of its fertility. Unless it is protected and its fertility restored, land that was once fruitful can become as barren as the surface of the moon.

Oceans

Earth is a watery planet. Water in the oceans covers more than 70 percent of its surface. Water is present on earth in three forms. It is solid when it freezes into ice, it is liquid as water, and it is a gas when it becomes invisible water vapor in the air.

The water that fills the ocean basins makes it possible for life on earth to exist. The heat of the sun evaporates water from the sea and turns it into water vapor.

The vapor rises and condenses to form clouds. The clouds bring moisture to the land as rain or snow. Without moisture there would be no life.

The oceans are never still. They are agitated by waves, tides, and CURRENTS. Warm currents bring mild weather to some regions, even those near the poles. Cold currents lower temperatures on the coasts they wash and chill onshore winds.

The great oceans

The four main bodies of water are the Pacific, Atlantic, Indian, and Arctic Oceans. Some people talk of a fifth ocean, the Southern, or Antarctic, Ocean. But most geographers regard the waters around Antarctica, the continent that surrounds the South Pole, as the southern parts of the Pacific, Atlantic, and Indian Oceans.

The oceans are all joined together. Each ocean contains seas, gulfs, and bays. Most of these areas of water are partly surrounded by land.

The ocean floor

Imagine that you can see clear through the deep ocean waters to the land that lies beneath, or that an ocean basin has been drained and that you have a bird's-eye view of it. Around the continents that border the ocean is a gently sloping zone called the continental shelf. The shelf is actually part of the continents.

At the edge of the shelf there is a very steep CONTINENTAL SLOPE, which falls sharply down to a flat plain, called the abyss.

The flat ocean floor is immense. It is broken by occasional volcanic mountains, or by lines of islands, some of which are topped by smoking volcanoes.

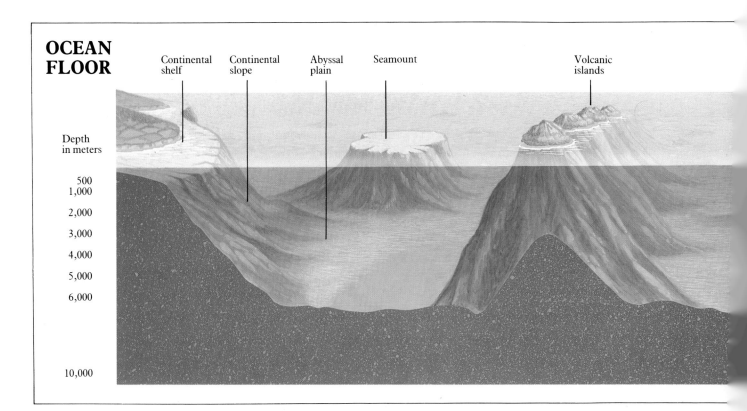

OCEAN FLOOR

Continental shelf   Continental slope   Abyssal plain   Seamount   Volcanic islands

Depth in meters

500
1,000
2,000
3,000
4,000
5,000
6,000

10,000

BIRTH OF AN OCEAN

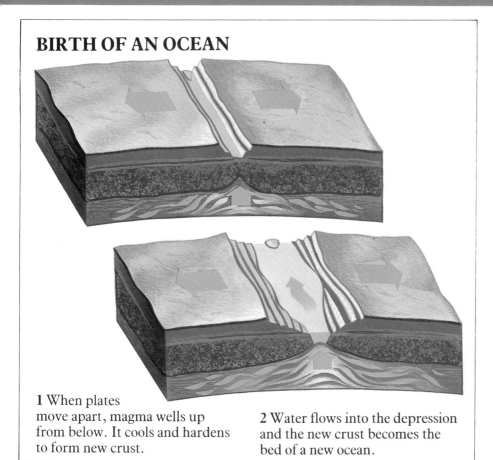

1 When plates move apart, magma wells up from below. It cools and hardens to form new crust.

2 Water flows into the depression and the new crust becomes the bed of a new ocean.

Running as far as the eye can see is a huge, broad mountain range. This is the ocean ridge. This massive range is sliced by narrow canyons and along its center is a long, deep valley.

Beyond the ridge lies more of the abyssal plain. Near the continent on the other side of the ocean is a colossal trench, so deep and dark that it seems the ocean bed is plunging into the earth's interior.

The spreading oceans

The trenches and ocean ridges mark the edges of the vast tectonic plates that form the cracked surface of the earth. The deep valley in the center of the ridge is a crack where new rock is being formed between two plates that are moving apart and widening the ocean. The ocean trench is where a plate is sliding down into the interior of the earth.

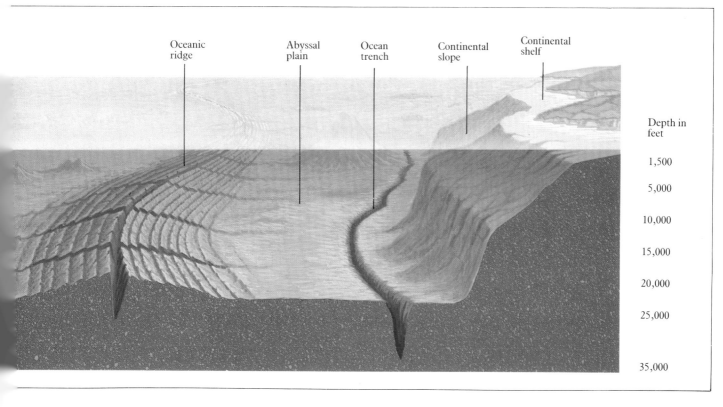

Oceanic ridge

Abyssal plain

Ocean trench

Continental slope

Continental shelf

Depth in feet

1,500

5,000

10,000

15,000

20,000

25,000

35,000

Tides

All along the coasts that border the oceans the level of the sea rises and falls, about twice a day. These rises and falls are called tides. High tide is when the water comes farthest up the beach. At low tide a lot more beach is exposed.

The moon and sun are responsible for tides. All heavenly bodies exert a pull on each other through the force of gravity. The moon's gravity exerts a pull on earth and everything upon it. Solid things such as buildings and mountains do not move enough to be detected, but the seas and oceans do. Their waters are drawn into two bulges on opposite sides of earth, one facing the moon, the other facing away from it. The moon drags the two bulges of water with it daily, as it circles earth.

Each time earth revolves, it takes an extra 50 minutes to catch up with the moon, so high tides occur 50 minutes later each day. The sun affects earth's tides in the same way as the moon, but to a lesser extent because it is much farther away.

Because oceans and seas differ in size, shape, and depth, their tides vary also. In some places there are tides twice a day, in some only once, and in others there are no tides.

Waves

Waves are movements of energy, but not matter. If you tie one end of a rope to a pole and move the other end up and down, you will see waves traveling along the rope. But the actual material of the rope does not move along.

At sea, waves begin as ripples caused by wind blowing over water. The wind whips the ripples up into waves. The size and power of a wave depend on the speed of the wind and the distance and length of time the wind has blown over the water. A wind blowing fast across a great mass of water builds up the biggest waves.

Out at sea, waves do not move water forward. Instead particles of water move around and around in small circles as the wave passes through. A cork in the sea bobs up and down, unless it is moved by the wind or a current.

When a wave reaches a sloping beach, the water drags on the seabed. The crests of the wave move closer together until the surface water topples forward and breaks on the seashore.

WIND AND WAVE

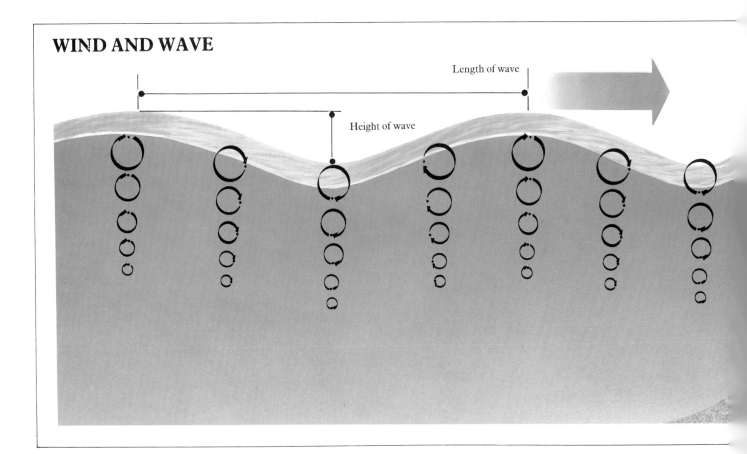

Length of wave

Height of wave

HIGH AND LOW

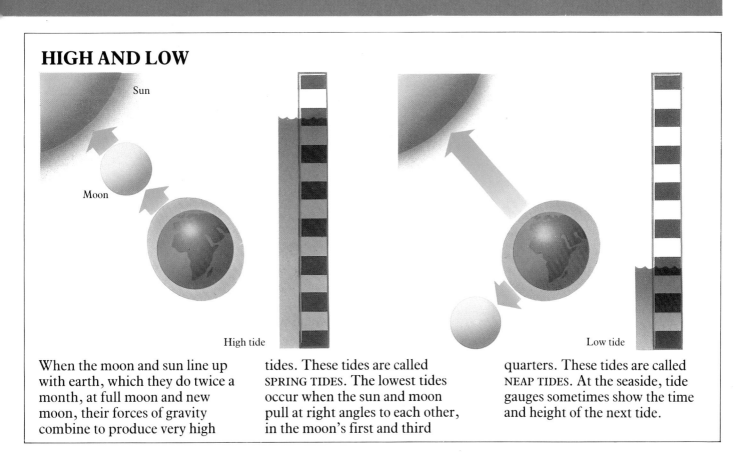

Sun

Moon

High tide

Low tide

When the moon and sun line up with earth, which they do twice a month, at full moon and new moon, their forces of gravity combine to produce very high tides. These tides are called SPRING TIDES. The lowest tides occur when the sun and moon pull at right angles to each other, in the moon's first and third quarters. These tides are called NEAP TIDES. At the seaside, tide gauges sometimes show the time and height of the next tide.

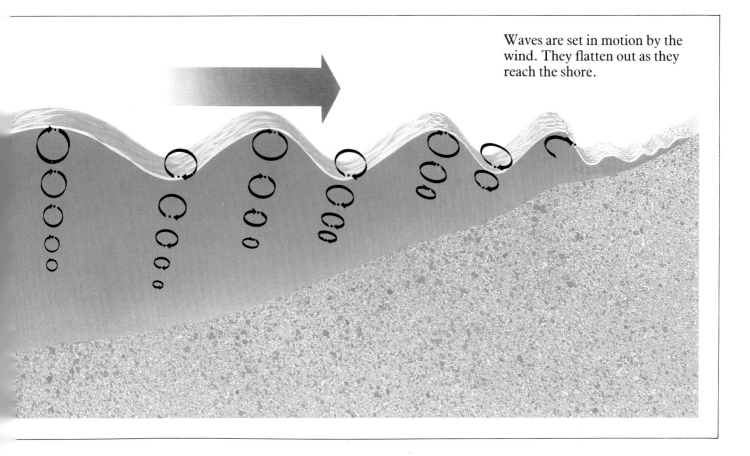

Waves are set in motion by the wind. They flatten out as they reach the shore.

Local and long-distance waves

If you see waves with steep sides and a choppy appearance, they are young waves that have been whipped up by local storms. If you are on a coast facing the open ocean, you may see waves that roll toward the land as a deep, heaving swell, with intervals of ten seconds or more between their peaks. As they reach shal-

Seawater

Unlike the water in rivers and most lakes, the water in the sea is saline (salty) and you cannot drink it. Animals that live in freshwater usually cannot live in the sea, and vice-versa.

Seawater freezes at a lower temperature. The temperature of seawater varies from 28°F (−2°C) (its freezing point) to almost 86°F

OCEAN CURRENTS

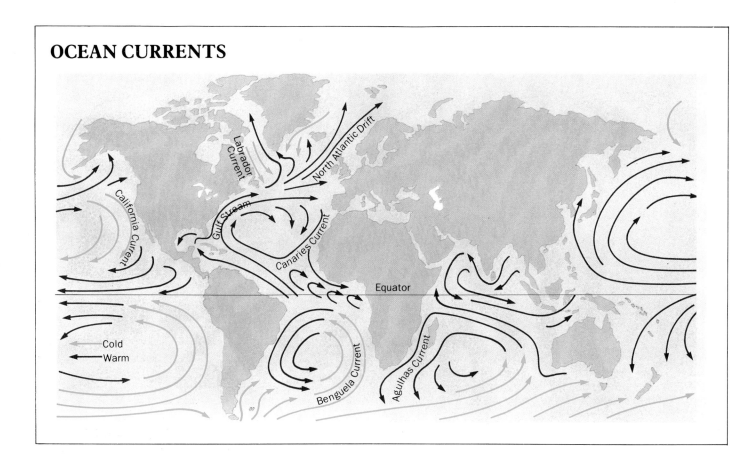

low water they rear up, curve forward, and crash onto the shore. Waves like these have traveled a long distance. For example, waves that break on the coast of California in summer may have begun during winter storms near New Zealand, and traveled some 6,200 miles (10,000 kilometers) across the Pacific Ocean.

(30°C) in warm, tropical seas. Much of the water in the polar regions is frozen. Saltwater is denser than freshwater, and cold water is denser than warm water.

The varying density of seawater is one of the reasons why the water of the oceans circulates continuously in currents. Cold water sinks; warm water rises to the surface.

The main ocean currents. Water retains heat more readily than land does, so warm ocean currents can bring warmth to lands that would otherwise be cold. For example, the coasts of Western Europe are heated by the North Atlantic Drift, a warm current that starts off the coast of Florida as the Gulf Stream. As a result Britain is much warmer than Newfoundland, which lies at the same latitude on the other side of the Atlantic.

Currents

The sun warms earth unevenly. About three times as much heat arrives at the equator as at the North and South Poles. Winds and ocean currents absorb heat in equatorial regions and lose it, little by little, as they move north and south toward cooler regions.

Prevailing winds, which blow steadily for most of the day and for most of the year, cause surface currents in the oceans. The rotation of earth causes the currents to veer from their paths. North of the equator they curve to the right, south of it to the left. Other currents flow deep down in the oceans, often in opposite directions to those on the surface.

Plankton

Nekton

Benthos

OCEAN FOOD WEB

PLANKTON is the basis of the ocean food web. PHYTOPLANKTON make their own food in the way that land plants do. They enrich the sea with oxygen and provide food for the swarms of plankton animals—the ZOOPLANKTON—including tiny shrimp called krill.

Fish, such as herring, feed on the zooplankton, and in their turn are eaten by cod, dolphins, sharks, tuna, and other bigger creatures that make up the free-swimming NEKTON. Certain whales also feed on plankton.

Scraps of dead plants and animals sink to the seabed. Some are eaten by bottom-living creatures (BENTHOS). The rest are broken down by BACTERIA into nutritious compost. Cold currents churn up these deposits and bring them to the surface, stimulating the rapid growth of plankton, which become food for vast shoals of fish.

Hot and cold currents

Submarine currents are caused by differences in water temperature. Continual cooling at the poles causes the water there to sink and flow toward the equator. Currents of warm water flow from the equator toward the poles over the top of the deeper water. The warm and cold currents form vast spirals of water on either side of the equator in the Pacific, Atlantic, and Indian Oceans.

The deep, cold water moves slowly. It may take hundreds of years on its journey to the equator, but in places, some of it comes to the surface. This happens when offshore winds push the top layer of water away from the land. The deep, cold water wells up to replace it and continues to drift toward the equator as surface currents.

Fishing

Cold currents bring nutritious food to the ocean surface, causing rapid growth in plankton that attract huge shoals of fish. Plankton is far more plentiful in cold waters than in warm, which is why the main fishing grounds of the world are in the Arctic and Antarctic.

Fish are a tremendously important source of food. Rich nations harvest tons and tons of fish that are processed in factory ships on the way back to port. People of poor countries depend on what they can catch themselves or buy in local markets. So much fish is taken from the sea that international regulations have to be enforced to prevent overfishing. Nets must have holes large enough to allow young fish to escape them, to have a chance of breeding and renewing FISH STOCKS. Fishing ships are allowed to fish only for fixed quotas.

TYPES OF NET

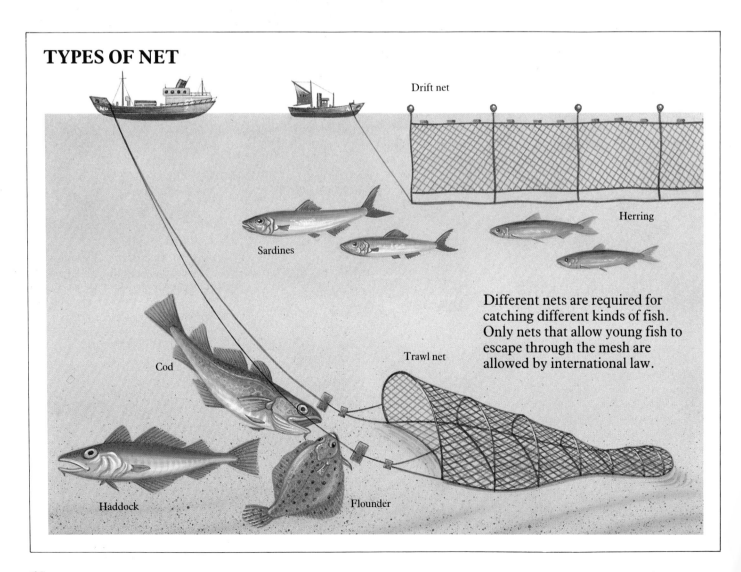

Drift net

Herring

Sardines

Cod

Haddock

Flounder

Trawl net

Different nets are required for catching different kinds of fish. Only nets that allow young fish to escape through the mesh are allowed by international law.

Power from the sea

The sea contains vast resources that people are only just beginning to exploit. Attempts are being made to use the ebb and flow of the tides as a source of energy. In a few places, such as the estuaries of the Rance River in France and the Annapolis River in Nova Scotia, Canada, the twice-daily movement of the tides is used to generate electricity.

Devices for harnessing wave power are being tested all the time, in a search for some that will provide an endless and economical source of power from the bobbing movements of the water. Another idea yet to operate commercially is to build thermal power stations, which will use the difference in temperature between the deep, cold water and the warm surface water to generate electricity.

Wealth from the sea

There are rich mineral deposits beneath the sea, and vast quantities of chemicals and minerals are dissolved in its waters. More than one-third of the world's oil comes from deposits deep under the seabed. Other minerals are mostly more difficult or expensive to extract. One exception is magnesium. Most of the world's supplies of this mineral come from the sea.

WEALTH FROM THE OCEANS

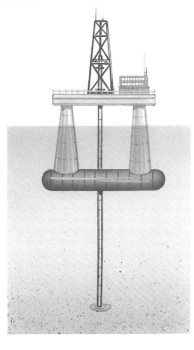

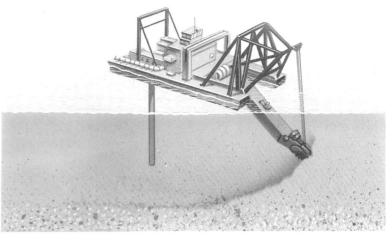

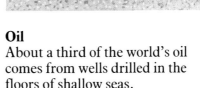

Oil
About a third of the world's oil comes from wells drilled in the floors of shallow seas.

Gravel and minerals
A dredger scoops up offshore sand and gravel. Minerals are also dredged in this way.

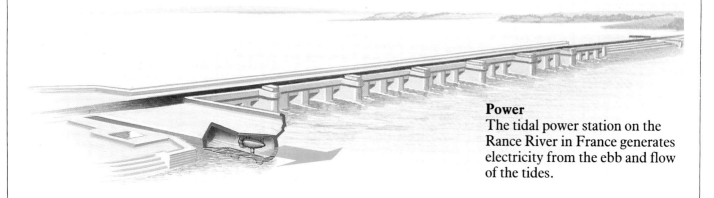

Power
The tidal power station on the Rance River in France generates electricity from the ebb and flow of the tides.

Rivers

Water is essential to life. From the beginning of human history, people have looked for sources of clean, fresh water and found them in rivers. Rivers provide water for drinking, for washing, and for growing crops. They provide a means of transporting people and goods. Great civilizations and great cities have grown up beside them.

From mountain to ocean

Even the greatest rivers start in a small way, as a thin trickle of water from a melting glacier or a tiny SPRING high in the mountains. Most rivers are born in the mountains and flow relentlessly down to the sea. Small or great, they follow much the same course. Their lives can be divided into three stages: youth, maturity, and old age.

Young river

In the mountains a river is young. It is narrow and flows swiftly over the rocks down relatively steep slopes. The running water carries pieces of rock that cut into the ground below and gouge out holes. The holes merge together, creating a lower riverbed. The river valley grows deeper and its sides are steep.

The mature river

Beyond the mountains the river valley becomes wider and its sides less steep. The river grows bigger as other small streams—TRIBUTARIES—flow into it, and water and eroded material from the land drain into it. Now in its mature stage, it flows more gently, though still vigorously. It swings from side to side across the valley floor in a series of curves called MEANDERS.

A melting glacier, or spring, is the source of the young river, which is fed by tributaries and rainfall, picking up sediment as it meanders through the valley.

Then, heavy with water and eroded material, it winds slowly across its floodplain. It dumps much of its load during floods. It dumps the rest at its life's end, in the sea.

Glacier

Valley

Floodplain

Estuary

BIRTH OF A RIVER

Rainwater sinks readily through the soil until it meets rock. If the rock is PERMEABLE, the water continues to sink through it until it meets a barrier of IMPERMEABLE rock. The water flows along the top of the impermeable layer until it seeps to the surface. There it may bubble out in one place as a spring, or lie on the surface, forming a marsh or a bog or even a lake.

The old river

As the land becomes flatter, the river slows down. It is now in its old age and nearing the end of its journey. Heavy with the water it has gathered, it winds across a flat plain. The plain is covered by grains of sand, rock, and clay the river has brought down over the centuries from the upper part of its course. What it does not dump on the land during floods, the river carries with it to the sea.

Rapids and waterfalls

The water of the young river flows swiftly down sloping channels, gouging out the riverbed as it goes. When the channel slopes steeply, the river forms rapids, flowing over the rocks and breaking up in clouds of spray.

Some rocks, such as granite, are hard and wear away very slowly. Soft rocks, such as clay and sandstone, wear away fairly quickly. When the river flows over a place where hard rock gives way to soft rock, the softer rock is worn away more quickly. The edge of the hard rock is left like a step, over which the river plunges in a waterfall or cascade.

As the water, with its load of rocks, hits the bottom, more of the soft rock is worn away and the fall becomes taller. The falling water and stones often gouge out a basin, called a PLUNGE POOL, at the foot of the waterfall.

Waterfalls occur where hard rock gives way to soft. Falling water cuts away the soft rock below, leaving the shelf of the waterfall unsupported.

Meandering along

In its mature stage, after it has left the hills, the river flows over gentle slopes. It continues to find the easiest path, which usually winds back and forth, so that the river swings from side to side in a series of S bends. When the river flows around a bend, the water and its load of mud and fine gravel swings toward the outside bank. Here the river is at its deepest and the water flows fastest. The river tends to wear away this bank.

On the opposite side, on the inner curve, the water flows more slowly and the river is shallower. The river drops part of its load as silt at the foot of this bank. Slowly the silt piles up and becomes part of the bank, which creeps farther and farther out into the river. As one bank wears away and the other is added to, the bend becomes bigger.

Lakes left behind

Sometimes a meander bend becomes a narrow loop, and the

RIVERS UNDERGROUND

When rain falls on hills and mountains, it mostly runs away in streams and rivers. But if the underlying rock is limestone, the rain sinks into it. Limestone is full of tiny cracks, through which the water seeps. Rainwater is not pure water. It has carbon dioxide from the air dissolved in it, which makes it slightly acidic. The acid is very weak, but little by little it can dissolve limestone.

Over thousands of years the acid eats away shafts and tunnels in the rock. Water collects in these tunnels and they become rivers underground, which run into huge caverns of limestone. Sometimes a stream on land disappears down a shaft and becomes an underground waterfall.

Stalactites and stalagmites

Sometimes water droplets that fall from the cavern roof to the floor leave deposits of rock particles. As the water continues to drip, more and more particles build up until a column of rock called a stalagmite is formed. The dripping water leaves similar deposits behind on the roof and these build up, too, to form a stalactite. Sometimes the two meet and form a solid column.

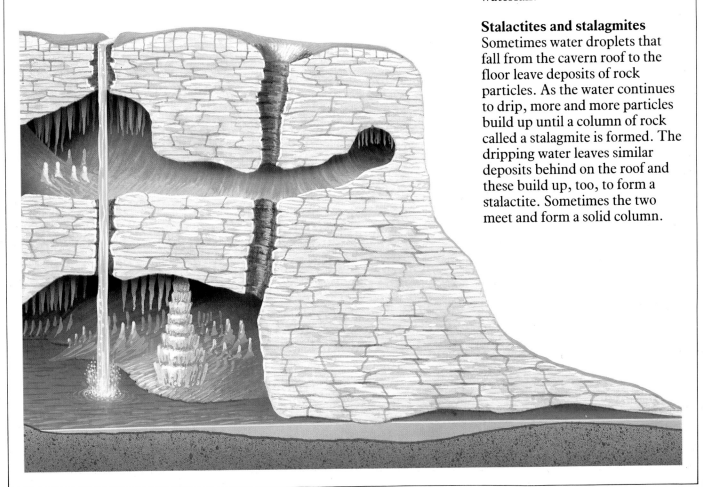

THE MATURE RIVER

You can see what happens to the bed of a meandering river (right). On the outside of each bend, the sides are steep; on the inside, the sediment piles up in a more gentle slope. This is because the current on the outside edge of each bend is faster than on the inside and wears away the riverbank so that it is almost like a cliff. On the inside, the bank grows out into the river. This makes the river swing from side to side (below).

river—perhaps during a flood—takes a shortcut across the neck of the loop. The new channel is a faster route so the river switches to it, leaving a cutoff loop that remains as a lake. A lake formed like this is called an OXBOW LAKE, a mortlake (literally "dead lake"), a bayou (in America), or a billabong (in Australia).

The floodplain

In old age, the river's work of erosion is done. Now it is adding to the flat land across which it flows. It deposits silt at its sides, building up embankments. Every so often, the river floods. It flows over its banks and deposits silt all over the surrounding floodplain. Floods may cause damage, but they also bring benefits. Before artificial fertilizers were available, farmers relied upon the layer of fresh, fertile soil that the river spread over their land.

Flooding is caused by rain for weeks on end or by sudden heavy storms. Some rivers that rise in high mountains flood every spring. The snow on the mountains melts so quickly that more water flows into the rivers than they can carry away. In Australia many riverbeds are dry for months, even years, on end. But rain many miles away can cause a flash flood. Water sweeps down the dry riverbed without warning and may drown people or animals in its way.

Trees and floods

Floods may be caused when forests are cut down on mountain slopes. Trees help to prevent floods. Their roots bind the soil, soak up water, and keep the soil from being washed away. Their leaves act as an umbrella, which breaks the force of the raindrops—an important factor in torrential rain.

The removal of trees increases the volume of water in the nearest rivers. Loose soil washes into the rivers, chokes them with mud, and causes floods downstream. Disastrous floods that occurred in Bangladesh in 1988 were the result of the destruction of millions of trees along the banks of the Ganges and Brahmaputra Rivers.

Journey's end

Most rivers carry huge loads of sediment. Any silt and sand that the river has not deposited in its final journey across the floodplain it dumps into the sea. It is

57

LEVEES

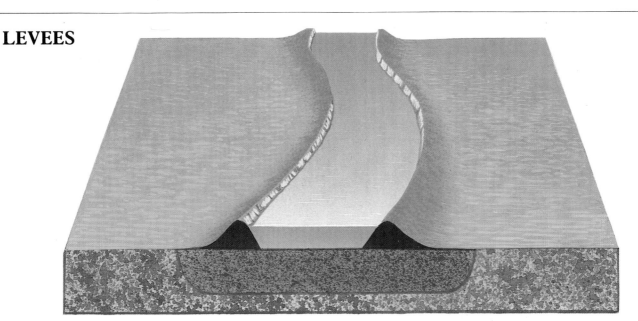

A river dumps heavier material along its banks. In time this material builds up into banks called LEVEES. The levees protect the land near the river from flooding. People often strengthen them artificially. Because a river also deposits silt in its bed, it may end up flowing between its levees above the level of the plain. Neither natural nor artificial levees were enough to hold back the swollen waters of the Mississippi River in 1993.

these sediments that will eventually become sedimentary rocks. If the river flows fast enough, a funnel-shaped ESTU-ARY develops and the sediments may be carried many miles from its mouth.

If the flow is not so fast, the sediments build up into a DELTA at the river mouth.

Deltas make good farmland. The soil is deep and fertile, and there are hardly any large rocks or stones in it, so it is easy to cultivate. Even if there is not much rainfall in the area, the river is close enough to provide sufficient freshwater for growing crops.

Although deltas attract people because of their rich soil, they are often dangerous places to live. Flat and scarcely above sea level, they are easily flooded by their own rivers or by high tides.

RIVER MOUTHS

Where tides and ocean currents are not strong enough to disperse the sediments, new land is formed. The river builds up a wedge-shaped area known as a delta. The river then cuts a series of streams through the delta to carry its water to the sea, instead of having a wide estuary.

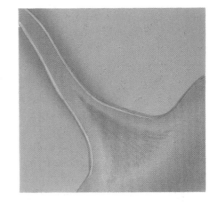

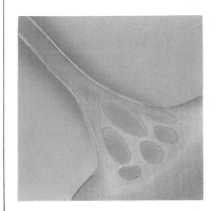

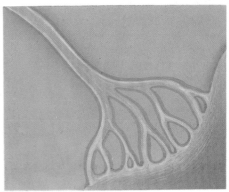

RIVERS MADE YOUNG—THE GRAND CANYON

Over millions of years rivers can wear down even the highest mountains to almost flat plains. The rivers then flow slowly in their old age. But land does not always stay the same. Sometimes spectacular changes take place that make an old river young again, a process called REJUVENATION.

Movements in the earth's crust push up new mountains and plateaus. If ICE CAPS increase, the sea level drops. When these things happen, the lazy old river must once again flow down steep slopes. The river acquires new energy to cut a deeper bed in the old river valley.

The outstanding example of the power of a rejuvenated river is the Grand Canyon in the United States. Ten million years ago the Colorado River meandered lazily over its broad floodplain, just above sea level. But the movements that created the Rocky Mountains gradually raised the floodplain by approximately 8,200 feet (2,500 meters).

As the land rose, the Colorado ran faster, because it had farther to fall before it reached the sea. As it did so, it began to carve out the canyon. The more the land rose, the deeper the canyon became. The river today still follows the same meandering course it did ten million years ago. But its canyon is 217 miles (350 kilometers) long, up to 12 miles (20 kilometers) wide, and in places nearly 1.2 miles (2 kilometers) deep. It is growing deeper at the rate of 0.3 inch (1 centimeter) every 70 years.

Ponds and lakes

Not all rivers flow into the sea. Some flow into ponds and lakes. Generally other streams take the water away again, but some lakes are the final deposit of river water. They include the Caspian and Aral Seas in Asia and the Dead Sea between Israel and Jordan. These "seas" are really lakes. Because they are in areas of high evaporation, the lakes are very salty. The Dead Sea is nine times as salty as the oceans.

Most lakes, especially in Europe and North America, formed when glaciers carved huge hollows in the rock. Finland has as many as 60,000 lakes, all formed in this way.

Faults may sometimes leave hollows where lakes can form. The Aral, Dead, and Caspian Seas were formed in this way, and so was the world's deepest lake, Baikal, in Siberia. Other lakes form in the craters of extinct volcanoes.

A lake survives as long as it receives a supply of water and its banks remain intact. But by their very nature lakes are short-lived—in geological terms. Their rivers dry up or are diverted, they fill with silt, and their banks are worn away.

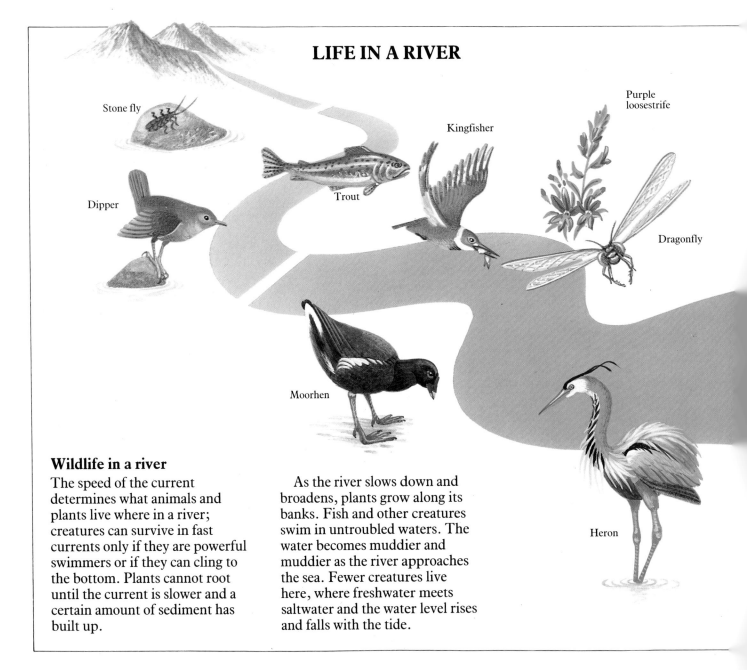

LIFE IN A RIVER

Stone fly

Dipper

Trout

Kingfisher

Purple loosestrife

Dragonfly

Moorhen

Heron

Wildlife in a river

The speed of the current determines what animals and plants live where in a river; creatures can survive in fast currents only if they are powerful swimmers or if they can cling to the bottom. Plants cannot root until the current is slower and a certain amount of sediment has built up.

As the river slows down and broadens, plants grow along its banks. Fish and other creatures swim in untroubled waters. The water becomes muddier and muddier as the river approaches the sea. Fewer creatures live here, where freshwater meets saltwater and the water level rises and falls with the tide.

Keeping rivers clean

Because rivers are so useful, they are often abused. The life in a river and the life on land that depends on the river exist in a delicate balance. Rivers are dammed to provide power and irrigation. Huge towns with growing populations use more and more water and return ever more waste to the river. Industries dump chemicals in the water. Fertilizers and pesticides from farmland drain into the river, causing overgrowth of waterweeds and the poisoning of water animals. As long as no one takes too much water from it or puts harmful substances in it, a river can maintain its own healthy balance. But many rivers have been used simply as drains, and pollution controls are urgently needed.

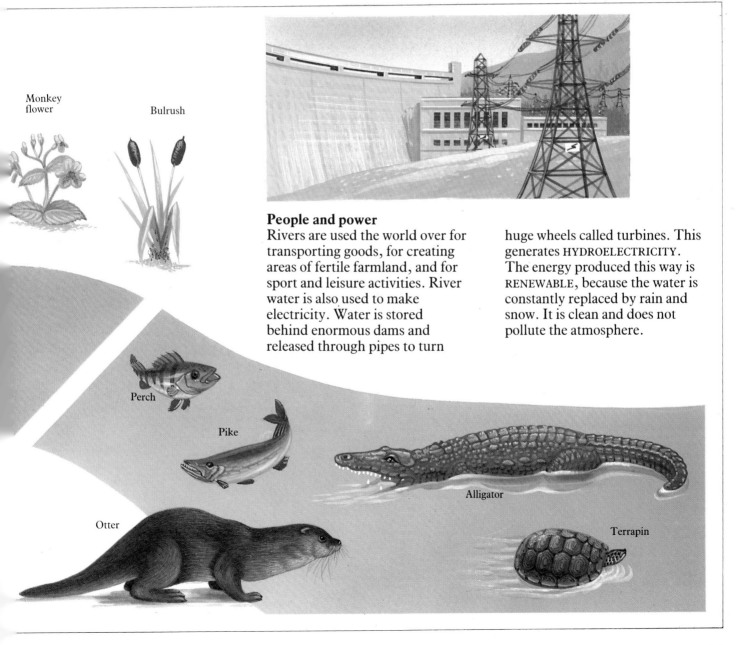

Monkey flower

Bulrush

People and power

Rivers are used the world over for transporting goods, for creating areas of fertile farmland, and for sport and leisure activities. River water is also used to make electricity. Water is stored behind enormous dams and released through pipes to turn huge wheels called turbines. This generates HYDROELECTRICITY. The energy produced this way is RENEWABLE, because the water is constantly replaced by rain and snow. It is clean and does not pollute the atmosphere.

Perch

Pike

Alligator

Otter

Terrapin

61

Weather and Climate

Earth is surrounded by a transparent atmosphere. This is a blanket of gases, hundreds of miles thick, held in place by gravity. The gases, which together we call air, are a mixture of NITROGEN and oxygen (which make up nearly 99 percent of the air) and ARGON (almost 1 percent) and variable but tiny amounts of carbon dioxide, HELIUM, hydrogen, and other gases. Air also contains invisible water vapor and microscopic particles of dust, POLLEN, and MICROBES.

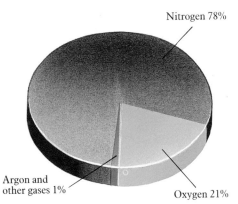

Nitrogen 78%

Argon and other gases 1%

Oxygen 21%

Nearly four-fifths of the air is nitrogen. Most of the rest is oxygen, with much smaller amounts of other gases.

The atmosphere is vital to life. As well as providing essential oxygen, the atmosphere prevents the heat of the sun from roasting earth during the day and keeps it warm by night by holding heat. During the day it is a sun shield and at night it is a blanket.

Air pressure

Although it is transparent and feels weightless, air has weight. It presses down on us all the time. We do not feel AIR PRESSURE because the pressure inside our bodies is the same as the pressure outside, and solid ob-

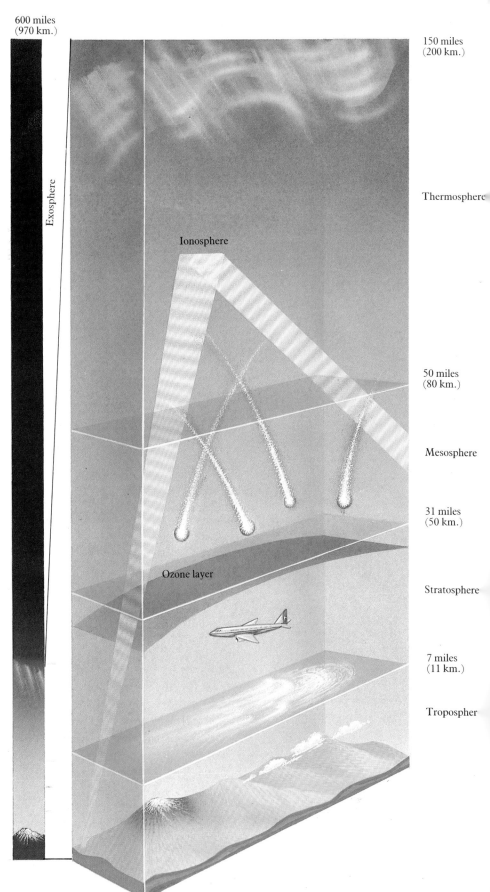

600 miles (970 km.)

Exosphere

150 miles (200 km.)

Thermosphere

Ionosphere

50 miles (80 km.)

Mesosphere

31 miles (50 km.)

Ozone layer

Stratosphere

7 miles (11 km.)

Troposphere

The layers of the atmosphere: The TROPOSPHERE is the layer of air in which we live. Our weather is confined to this layer, which grows cooler with height. Airplanes often fly above the weather in the thin air of the STRATOSPHERE, which also contains the OZONE LAYER. The outer layers of the atmosphere are the MESOSPHERE (where meteor trails can be seen), the THERMOSPHERE, and the EXOSPHERE, which merges into space. The lowest level of the thermosphere, called the IONOSPHERE, reflects radio waves back to earth.

jects are heavier than air. The total weight of the atmosphere is about 5.2 trillion tons.

With all that weight, pressure at the bottom of the atmosphere is higher than it is farther out from earth. Pressure falls very rapidly as you climb a mountain and the air becomes thinner and lighter.

Atmospheric layers

The atmosphere can be divided into layers. The lowest level is the troposphere, which holds 90 percent of the atmosphere's gases. Above it are the stratosphere, mesosphere, and thermosphere, where the air gradually becomes thinner. Beyond them is the exosphere, where there is virtually no air at all.

Ozone

A form of oxygen called OZONE is present in the atmosphere in small amounts. There is a vital layer of ozone in the ionosphere which protects us from the harmful ULTRAVIOLET rays of the sun. It is these rays that cause the skin to tan and burn and can cause cancer of the skin. The ozone layer shields the earth from over 95 percent of these rays. Many

scientists think that chlorofluorocarbons (CFCs) and other pollutants that we carelessly discharge into the atmosphere are damaging the ozone layer and causing GLOBAL WARMING.

The greenhouse effect

The GREENHOUSE EFFECT of the atmosphere keeps the earth warm. The sun's INFRARED heat rays can pass through the atmosphere, just as they can pass

through the glass in a greenhouse. The rays heat the air, the plants, and everything else in a greenhouse, but the glass walls hold the heat in, allowing it to escape only slowly. Without the atmosphere to hold warm air near the earth's surface, the temperature on earth would be much, much cooler.

When the infrared rays do gradually escape from earth, they rise into the atmosphere, but they do not all pass out of the

atmosphere. They are absorbed by carbon dioxide and other gases. The more carbon dioxide there is in the atmosphere, the more heat is retained. Carbon dioxide is given off in our breath, by the burning of fossil fuels, and by many industrial processes.

Temperature

Different parts of the world receive different amounts of heat from the sun. The amount of

heat depends upon latitude—distance from the equator—and the time of the year. At high latitudes, a similar amount of the sun's rays is spread over a greater surface area than at the equator because of the curve of the earth. The rays also have to travel through a greater thickness of atmosphere. The tilt of the earth and the annual revolution of the earth around the sun are responsible for the seasonal temperature changes.

GREENHOUSE EFFECT

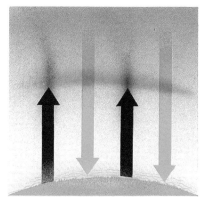

The atmosphere acts like a greenhouse, keeping the earth warm by holding a layer of warm air near the earth's surface. Too

much carbon dioxide increases the greenhouse effect, so that extra heat is trapped.

WAYS OF THE WINDS

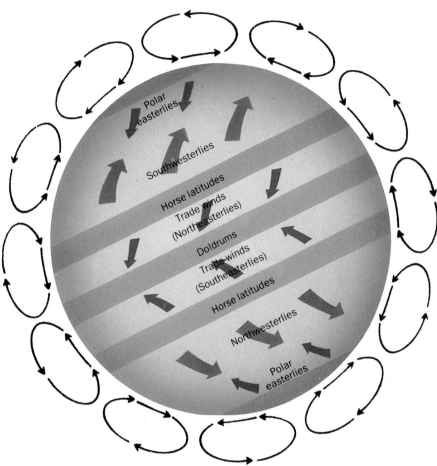

Polar easterlies
Southwesterlies
Horse latitudes
Trade winds (Northeasterlies)
Doldrums
Trade winds (Southeasterlies)
Horse latitudes
Northwesterlies
Polar easterlies

Winds blow from areas of high pressure to areas of low pressure. Hot air at the equator rises and creates areas of low air pressure, called the DOLDRUMS. The rising air cools and spreads out to the north and south, where it sinks and becomes warmer, causing areas of high pressure called the HORSE LATITUDES. The warm air flows toward the equator in winds called the TRADE WINDS.

Moving air

The unequal heating of the earth's surface causes movements of air—winds. Warm air at the equator moves toward the poles, and cold air at the poles moves toward the equator. In addition, the earth's rotation deflects the winds (to the right in the northern hemisphere, and to the left in the southern).

This regular wind pattern, however, is complicated because the earth's surface is made up of land and water. Land heats up more quickly than water, but it also loses its heat more quickly. This sets up differences in pressure in different parts of the world. Great masses of air (AIR MASSES) push one another around the atmosphere, rising, falling, being warmed or cooled, picking up moisture, or shedding it.

The water cycle

Water is as vital to life as air. Like the air, water is continually on the move. More than 99 percent of all the water on earth is in the oceans or locked in the polar ice caps. The remaining 1 percent is constantly being exchanged between the land and the sea in an endless circulation called the WATER CYCLE.

The water cycle is powered by the sun. The sun's heat evaporates water from the surface of the oceans. This water turns into invisible vapor, which "vanishes

THE WATER CYCLE

into thin air" and is swept away by winds. When moisture-laden winds cross high ground, they are forced upward into cooler regions of the atmosphere. As the air rises, it cools and can no longer hold all its water vapor. The vapor condenses, turning back into water in the form of very tiny droplets (or ice crystals if it is very cold).

Masses of droplets or ice crystals form clouds. In time the droplets merge to form larger drops. These are the raindrops that fall to land when it rains. Ice crystals form snowflakes. As they fall, snowflakes may turn back into droplets if the air through which they pass is warm enough. Otherwise they fall to land as snow.

Back to the sea

Water vapor does not only rise over mountains. It rises over the sea, too, if there is an upward-moving current of warm air to lift it. Nearly three-quarters of the water evaporated from the oceans falls back into them as rain or snow.

The remaining quarter falls on land. Some runs straight into rivers, but most of it falls onto soil, which soaks it up like a sponge. The water seeps through the soil and into the rocks below. This water eventually finds its way back into a river, which then begins its travels back to the sea, where its journey began.

Some water remains trapped under the ground in porous rocks for a very long time, hundreds, sometimes thousands of years. Such water is called GROUND-WATER.

The water cycle is a continuous circulation of water, evaporating from the oceans, being carried to the land and dumped, then flowing in rivers and in underground rocks back to the sea.

Climate

The climate of an area is its general pattern of weather over a long period of time. It is the average of many small variations. Near the equator the hot weather varies so little throughout the year that it is the climate, just as the cold weather at the poles remains the same.

Temperatures generally increase toward the equator, but latitude is not the only factor in determining climate. Temperatures are also affected by altitude (they decrease with height), by ocean currents (which increase or decrease the temperature of coastal lands), and by distance from the sea (inland areas have warmer summers and colder winters than coastal areas).

Rainfall also varies from place to place. The wettest regions are generally those reached by winds that have blown far across the sea. The winds dump their rain on the coastal mountains. When the air has crossed the mountains, it sinks down, getting warmer and picking up moisture.

Deserts

In some hot regions winds sweeping down from coastal ranges have dried the land so much that deserts have developed, where there is less than 10 inches (25 centimeters) of rain per year. Deserts also occur in the heart of continents that no rain-bearing winds ever reach. Deserts are not all hot. Parts of Siberia, Canada, and Alaska near the North Pole receive virtually no rain or snow. The world's largest hot deserts occur in two separate bands that stretch between latitudes 15° and 40° North and South.

Equatorial regions

Pressure is high in deserts but low in EQUATORIAL regions. In equatorial lowlands temperatures rise to about 86°F (30°C) every day and there are virtually no seasons. The hot air is laden with moisture. Thick clouds form and by late afternoon every day, thunderstorms bring torrential rain (called CONVECTION RAIN) that lasts into the night. In this hothouse atmosphere a vast number and variety of trees and other plants grow up, vying for light and space.

Mountainous regions

As you climb a mountain, the air gets colder. The temperature drops by about 35°F (2°C) for every 660 feet (200 meters) you ascend. The reason for this is that the air is thinner higher up. As a result there are fewer particles of dust and moisture in it to trap and give out the heat from the sun. The clearer mountain air captures less warmth from the sun's rays than the dustier, moister air lower in the valleys. Even on the equator, where the climate is hotter than anywhere else, the tallest mountains, such as Mount Kenya, are snowcapped.

Temperate regions

In TEMPERATE lands there are rarely extremes of temperature or rainfall, but seasonal changes are marked. Because temperate regions are not too hot or too cold, too wet or too dry, they are good for growing crops and grazing animals. People who live in temperate zones enjoy a higher standard of living than those who live elsewhere in the world, where climatic conditions make agriculture more difficult.

WEATHER FEATURES

Clouds

Different kinds of clouds form at different levels in the atmosphere. They are named after their shapes. Flat layers of clouds are called STRATUS. Low gray stratus clouds bring dull weather and darken to bring rain. Fluffy white CUMULUS clouds are a sign of fine weather but may grow bigger and darker into rain clouds or thunderclouds. CIRRUS clouds, often called mares' tails because of the way they curl, form high up and warn of changing weather.

Thunderstorms

Thunderstorms occur when warm, moist air is forced upward by AIR CURRENTS or by a mass of cold air burrowing under a mass of warm air. The worst thunderstorms occur almost daily in equatorial lands. Lightning is caused by electrical activity in the storm cloud. It is a giant spark. The spark heats the air, which expands rapidly and causes a clap or rumble of thunder.

Monsoons

MONSOONS are winds that blow over the Indian Ocean. For half the year they blow in a southwesterly direction; for the other half they blow in the reverse direction. The southwesterly monsoon brings torrential rain to India and surrounding areas from April until October.

Hurricanes

HURRICANES are whirling storms that start over tropical seas. They are also called tropical cyclones, typhoons, and willy-willies. Hot, moist air rises and forms clouds. Instead of cooling, the condensing water vapor produces heat and the air rises higher. Winds rush in to fill the void left by the rising air and create a whirlpool of air spiraling inward, ever faster, into an area of low

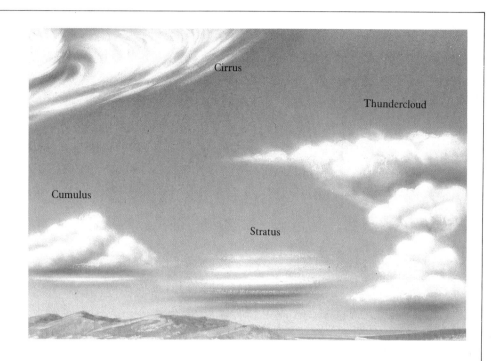

pressure. Here, in the eye of the storm, the air is still and clear, but around it winds may be tearing at speeds of 200 mph (320 kmh). When a moving hurricane reaches land, it begins to slow down and blow itself out – but usually after it has done enormous damage. Huge waves called hurricane surges rear up as high as 30 feet (9 meters) and wash over coasts. Wind, rain, and flooding devastate the land.

Tornadoes

A TORNADO is more violent than a hurricane, but smaller. As clouds condense, a funnel of air is sucked up into the sky. Winds whirl at speeds up to 500 mph (800 kmh), as the funnel twists its way across the land, leaving a swathe of damage behind, as much as 1,312 feet (400 meters) wide. Tornadoes that form over the sea are called WATERSPOUTS.

Earth – Past, Present, and Future

The universe is at least 16 billion years old. Earth is much younger, a mere 4.6 billion years old. Earth and its fellow planets were probably formed from a cloud of gases and dust that spun out from the sun. Under the force of gravity, the material formed into clumps that became the planets.

The first oceans

The newly formed earth was boiling hot. Heavy substances gravitated toward the center, lighter ones to the outside. The surface was covered with volcanoes, which, for millions of years, spouted gas and water vapor into the atmosphere. All the time the planet was cooling. Gradually, as it cooled, the thick cloud of water vapor condensed into rain. Water poured from the skies in a mighty deluge that lasted for thousands of years. It filled hollows in the earth's crust and formed the first oceans.

Earth's atmosphere at first consisted largely of nitrogen (still the main component), plus a mixture of other gases, including carbon dioxide, CHLORINE, METHANE, and AMMONIA. The only oxygen on earth was in the oceans (water is two parts hydrogen and one part oxygen).

Oxygen and life

Without oxygen no life is possible, so life could only begin in the sea. The earliest forms of life were the simplest of single-celled ORGANISMS (by comparison, a human body contains ten billion cells). The organisms extracted oxygen from the water, just as ocean plants and animals do today. The oxygen bubbled up to the surface of the water and escaped to become "free oxygen."

A FOSSIL FORMS

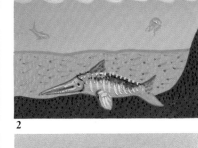

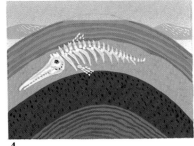

1 Millions of years ago a fish died and sank to the seabed.
2 The soft parts of its body decayed and sediment covered its bones.

3 The bones dissolved and were replaced by minerals from the water. The surrounding sediments hardened into rock.
4 Years later, earth movements

Some of the oxygen occurred in the form known as ozone. This ozone acted as a shield to protect the earth from the harmful ultraviolet rays of the sun.

Once enough ozone existed, it was possible for primitive multi-celled plants to push above the surface of the water without being burned up by the sun. Green plants produce oxygen as part of a process called PHOTOSYNTHESIS. They take in water, minerals, and carbon dioxide and, in the presence of sunlight, make food for themselves. In this way they harness the energy of the sun and produce food and life-giving oxygen.

The release of this gas transformed the atmosphere. As more and more plants evolved, more carbon dioxide was consumed and more oxygen produced. The amount of oxygen in the atmosphere gradually built up to its present level, about 21 percent. This meant that there was enough oxygen for land animals to exist. Animals take in oxygen and breathe out carbon dioxide during the process of respiration.

Evolution

During the millions of years of earth's history plants and animals have changed in an unending process called EVOLUTION. One kind of living thing has evolved into another. Fish have given rise to amphibians, amphibians to reptiles, reptiles to birds and mammals. Millions of different SPECIES (types) of animal

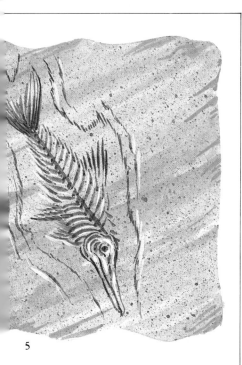

5

lifted the rocks and the fossil out of the sea.

5 The fossil itself was found on dry land when the rock was worn away to expose it.

and plants have inhabited the earth. From fossils, we know about the ones that lived on earth before human beings evolved.

Fossils

Fossils are the remains or traces of animals and plants that lived long ago. They have been preserved in sedimentary rocks. A fossil may be a shell, a bone, a tooth, or a skeleton. It may be a footprint, a worm's burrow, or a faint impression of a leaf.

When an animal dies, its body rots or is eaten. The soft parts decay first, followed by the skeleton or the shell. Sometimes the body or part of it is preserved, and a fossil results. Fossils form in a variety of ways. A skeleton on the seabed or the bottom of a lake can be quickly covered with sediment. Over thousands and millions of years the sediment hardens into rock.

At the same time the skeleton may be PETRIFIED—turned into stone. The original material of the bones dissolves away, but minerals carried in water pass through pores (tiny holes) in the bone, and gradually replace it all. The resulting stone skeleton is often harder than the surrounding rock.

Only the fossilized footprints of this coelurosaur were found. But they tell more about the animal than you might think—how heavy it was, how long its stride was, whether it was a plant-eater or a meat-eater, and so on.

Buried alive

Fewer fossils develop on land because there is less chance of a body being completely buried. However, many specimens have been found of creatures that have fallen into swamps or TAR PITS or have been buried by sandstorms. Whole "forests" of petrified trees have been found.

know that the rock is about the same age. The rocks above may have younger or older fossils. If they are older, the geologist will know that an upheaval has taken place.

Geological time

Geologists divide the history of the earth into eras and periods

ICE AGES

A number of times during the earth's history the climates of the world have grown intensely cold. Great sheets of ice—like the ice that covers the polar regions today—spread out over the land and covered areas that today are tropical. The ice sheets moved like glaciers, gouging and scraping the soil from the land and dumping it farther south in the Northern Hemisphere and farther north in the Southern.

These periods are known as ICE AGES, or glacial periods. The ice ages that we know most about occurred during the Quaternary period, when the ice advanced and retreated about 17 times. The ice ages lasted for up to 100,000 years, with warmer interglacial periods between them that lasted for about 10,000 years.

The last glacial period is known as the Great Ice Age. It began about 55 million years ago. Ice covered about a quarter of the land. Ice in North America came as far south as New York City and in Europe as far south as London. Today only about one-tenth of the land is covered with ice. Scientists disagree as to whether or not the Great Ice Age is over. We may be living at the beginning of an interglacial period or the end of a glacial.

Record of the rocks

To the geologist, the layers of sedimentary rocks are like the pages of a history book. But because of earth movements, erosion, and weathering, the book is difficult to read. The pages are often torn, turned upside down, scattered over a wide area, or, in many places, simply missing.

Fossils help geologists date the rocks. If they find a fossil of an animal that lived 200 million years ago in a rock layer, they

according to the age of the rocks. The oldest fossils (of bacteria) are about 3.5 billion years old and are found in rocks formed before the start of the Paleozoic era, during Precambrian times. Fossils are rare from this time because the earliest creatures had soft bodies that decayed quickly.

Extinction

We know from fossils that a vast array of living things has inhabited the earth. Many species,

AGES OF EARTH

Paleozoic era

At the beginning of the Cambrian period, there was an explosion of life in the warm seas that covered most of the earth. Worms, sponges, corals, starfish, GRAPTOLITES, and TRILOBITES all evolved.

Toward the end of the Cambrian, the first fish evolved. More and more new forms of fish and other sea creatures appeared during the Ordovician, Silurian, and Devonian periods. The first land plants appeared about the beginning of the Devonian and began to spread over the barren land. Toward the end of the Devonian some fish became able to breathe in air as well as in water. From them amphibians developed. They could live on land, but not far from the water in which they still had to lay their eggs.

During the Carboniferous period huge forests grew up of giant species of TREE FERNS, HORSETAILS, and CLUB MOSSES, quite different from their small modern relatives. These forests decayed and became the layers of coal that now mostly lie deep underground.

The great event in the Carboniferous period was the evolution of reptiles, the first animals that could live away from water because their eggs had hard shells. In the Permian period many more reptiles appeared. Some species of sea creatures, including the trilobites, became extinct.

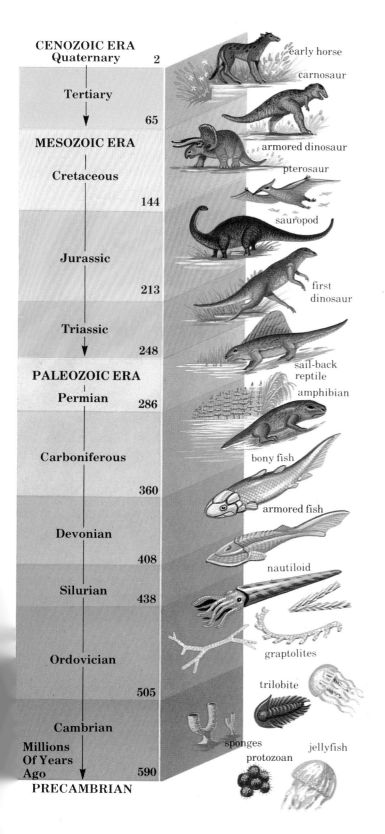

CENOZOIC ERA
Quaternary — 2

Tertiary

65

MESOZOIC ERA

Cretaceous

144

Jurassic

213

Triassic

248

PALEOZOIC ERA

Permian — 286

Carboniferous

360

Devonian

408

Silurian — 438

Ordovician

505

Cambrian

Millions
Of Years
Ago — 590

PRECAMBRIAN

early horse

carnosaur

armored dinosaur

pterosaur

sauropod

first
dinosaur

sail-back
reptile

amphibian

bony fish

armored fish

nautiloid

graptolites

trilobite

sponges

protozoan

jellyfish

Mesozoic era

More and more reptiles evolved during the Triassic period, including the first dinosaurs. Tiny mammals appeared, too. Creatures called AMMONITES evolved in the sea.

During the next period, the Jurassic, huge SAUROPOD dinosaurs, such as *Diplodocus* and *Brachiosaurus*, evolved. Above the heads of these peaceful plant-eaters flew winged reptiles, called PTEROSAURS, and the first birds.

The Cretaceous period saw even more dinosaurs, including the fierce CARNOSAURS, among them *Tyrannosaurus rex*.

At the end of the era, there was a mass extinction of animals, including the dinosaurs, large sea reptiles called PLESIOSAURS, and the ammonites. Nobody knows why so many species died out. But there must have been a change in climate because creatures equipped to withstand low temperatures survived.

Cenozoic era

MAMMALS and birds were the most important kinds of animals after the great extinction. Horses, elephants, apes, and many other kinds of animals appeared, including all those species alive today.

During the Quaternary period human beings evolved.

including the great dinosaurs, have become EXTINCT (died out). More, including perhaps the giant panda, will become extinct as their natural HABITATS are removed to make way for more human settlements and agricultural land.

Conserving wildlife

In the past many species were made extinct as a result of hunting. Scientists think that the woolly mammoth that lived during the ice ages was wiped out by the first humans. In later times bison were hunted for food and for their hides. But the great herds that once roamed the PRAIRIES were reduced far more by the activities of farmers who transformed the natural habitat into fields of wheat.

Today national parks have been set up in many countries where animals and plants can flourish undisturbed—except by tourists. Whales and fish stocks are protected by strict international laws, though not all countries abide by them.

Attempts to conserve endangered species are not always successful. Banning the sale of ivory from elephants' tusks, for instance, has resulted in such a

SPREADING DESERTS

In parts of Africa, where too many people have to eke a living from the parched land, animals strip the scrubby vegetation of its scanty foliage. People cut down the trees and bushes for firewood. The roots die, and the soil crumbles and blows away, leaving a desert in which nothing will grow.

Other humanmade deserts are in the making in southern Europe, where people have been clearing land of its protective vegetation for hundreds of years.

COMBATING POLLUTION

Probably the most urgent need for people living in industrialized countries is to clean up the environment by fighting pollution in all its forms. Pollution, which affects land, sea, and air equally, threatens the lives and livelihoods of people all around the world.

1 Rivers are often used as drains to carry away untreated sewage and factory and farm wastes. Damming of rivers brings benefits but also drawbacks. The dam traps fertile silt and deprives farmlands and fisheries of nutrients. Diseases may breed in the stagnant lake.
2 Towns and cities take water from rivers but also return it to them. Human and vegetable waste decays quickly; suitably treated, it can be disposed of in rivers, but only if the population is not too great. Exhaust from motor vehicles, chemicals, and

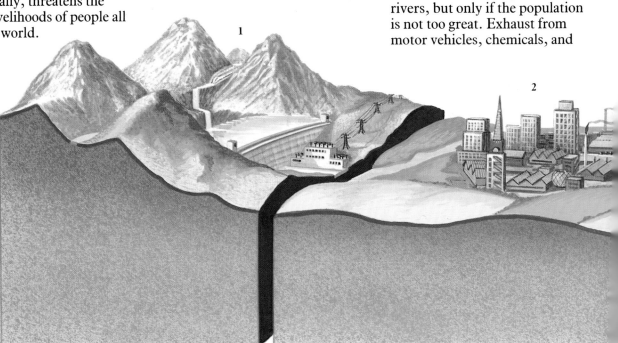

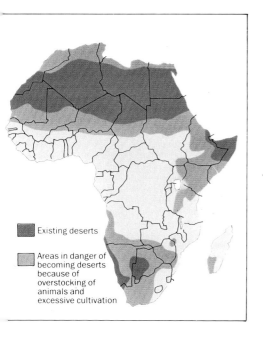

Existing deserts

Areas in danger of becoming deserts because of overstocking of animals and excessive cultivation

great increase in the elephant population in some areas of Africa that the vegetation will no longer support the herds, and animals are dying. Elephants are also killed inhumanely by poachers for the now illegal trade in ivory. Many conservationists feel that licensed hunting of elephants is a better alternative.

The living soil

Soil is composed of particles of minerals and decayed plant and animal matter. It is this that makes it fertile. The thin layer of soil that covers the land is precious, but it is vulnerable to weathering and erosion. When the natural vegetation is cleared, and there are no longer plant roots to absorb rainwater and hold the soil in place, wind and water can strip away the soil in no time. Farmers use CONTOUR PLOWING and TERRACING to prevent soil erosion.

Deserts in the making

Many areas of the world are unsuitable for growing crops but can support grazing animals such as cattle and sheep. Most of these areas are fairly dry and there is always a danger of overgrazing, especially in times of drought.

industrial waste poison the air we breathe. Some cities exist in a permanent SMOG caused by pollution.
3 Poisonous chemicals and gases are widely used in modern factories, and cleansing the waste is expensive. In most countries it is illegal to dump the waste, but sometimes the law is disregarded, with disastrous results.
4 Agriculture can be a source of pollution. Fertilizers washed into rivers cause water plants to flourish, sometimes so much that they clog up rivers completely. Pesticides not only kill pests on the land but also fish and other wildlife in rivers. Intensive farming also robs the soil of its fertility and may lead to DESERTIFICATION.
5 More and more water is taken from rivers to irrigate the land and make crops grow. The Colorado, for example, is a mighty river as it flows through the Grand Canyon, but by the time it reaches the Pacific Ocean it has lost so much water that it has become a trickle only a few feet wide.
6 Barges, oil tankers, and other ships empty their bilge tanks and spill oil into rivers and the sea, killing fish, birds, and plants. A major oil spillage not only destroys local wildlife but threatens the entire ocean food chain.
7 Nuclear power is clean but accidents may bring disastrous consequences. The explosion of a nuclear reactor or careless disposal of waste could release RADIOACTIVE FALLOUT that would last for generations.

3

4

5

6

7

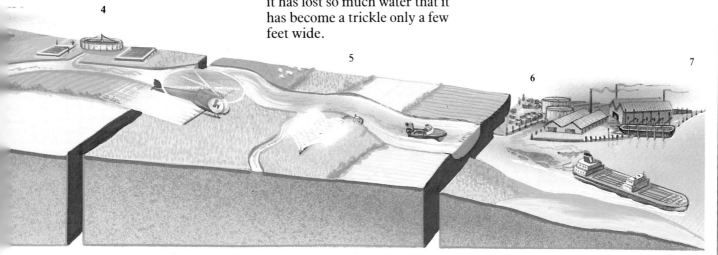

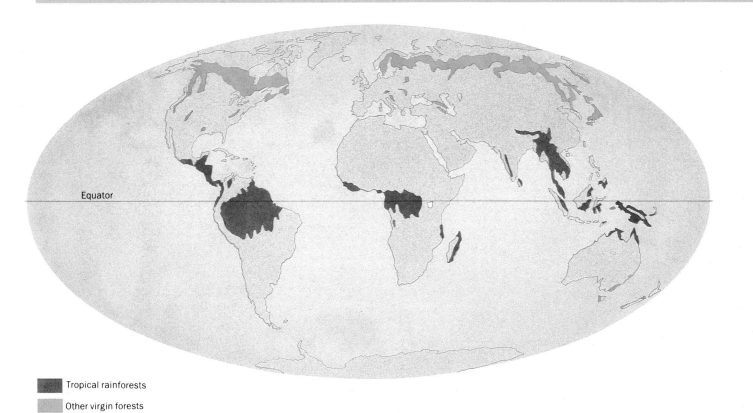

Equator

■ Tropical rainforests

▨ Other virgin forests

Forests

Many of the world's greatest forests were cut down centuries ago. The trees provided wood for fuel and timber for building homes. The cleared land provided fertile farmland. Today people are planting new forests— mostly of fast-growing CONIFERS (which provide SOFTWOOD)—and attempting to prevent the destruction of any more VIRGIN FOREST, especially the great tropical rain forests where HARDWOOD trees grow.

These rain forests contain more species of plants and animals than any other part of the world. They soak up the rain that falls on them, each giant tree absorbing hundreds of gallons of water a day, and putting about half of it back into the atmosphere through its leaves. This helps to keep the rainfall high.

The trees absorb a great deal of carbon dioxide, one of the main gases blamed for the slow rise in the earth's temperature. They give off oxygen, the gas we need to breathe.

The rain forests lie in three regions close to the equator. More than half are in South and Central America, a quarter in Southeast Asia, and the rest in central Africa. They are all in poor countries where people need more farmland to feed their populations and the money that comes from selling timber to richer countries.

Because rain forest conservation is important for the whole world, many people feel that international efforts must be made to prevent further destruction. This means compensating local people and providing them with a means of survival that does not depend on the trees.

The world's natural vegetation has been altered beyond recognition by the demands of humans. Most of the world was once covered by forest. Now areas of virgin forest are confined to a few inaccessible areas. International efforts are now being made to prevent the destruction of the remaining areas of rain forest.

It is not only forests that are disappearing. The world's resources of fuels and metals, such as iron, nickel, and LEAD, are also running out. Known oil reserves will not last another century. Finding alternative, nonpolluting sources of energy and resources is of vital importance to future generations.

Conflicting demands

In many places like the rain forests, there are conflicting needs. Poor people desperately need to cut down trees for fuel and they need more land on which to grow crops. Other people want to conserve the natural vegetation. Governments construct huge dams to bring much-needed water to dry lands. The water transforms barren land into farmland, but the flooding of the land behind the dam destroys the habitat and displaces people and wildlife.

Pollution of air and water

People in developed countries enjoy a high standard of living. Most of us have plenty of food, good homes, cars, and leisure facilities. The industrial development that has brought this about has also led to drawbacks, many of which reduce the quality of people's lives in ways that were not foreseen. Factories and cars emit smoke and pollutants into the atmosphere, making city air unhealthy to breathe. Controls

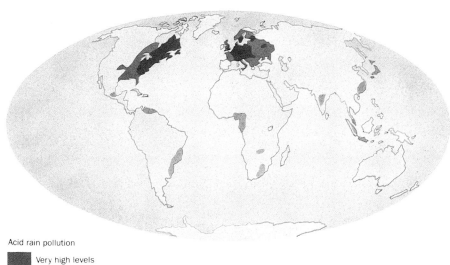

Acid rain pollution

■ Very high levels

■ High levels

Increasing levels

Millions of acres of forest have been badly damaged in Europe and North America, where levels of acid rain pollution have long been high. Now levels of pollution are rising alarmingly in other parts of the world.

are being enforced that reduce factory emissions and exhaust fumes from cars, but the problem will not be solved easily.

Factories also dump waste products in rivers and streams. In most developed countries, there are strict controls; dumping is illegal, but it still goes on. Farmers use fertilizers on their fields and these pollute rivers. Pesticides and other chemicals also end up in rivers.

In less-developed countries overpopulation and poverty are dangers to rivers. The Ganges River in India remained remarkably clean for centuries, but today more than 200 million people live in its basin. The river cannot cope with the great mass of waste it receives daily and it has become a health hazard to all who use it. But how can the people earn the money for expensive sewage systems?

How much have we got?

Air and water continuously renew themselves in great cycles. But other resources are not renewable. Energy comes from the sun and from the burning of substances formed over millions of years by natural processes—

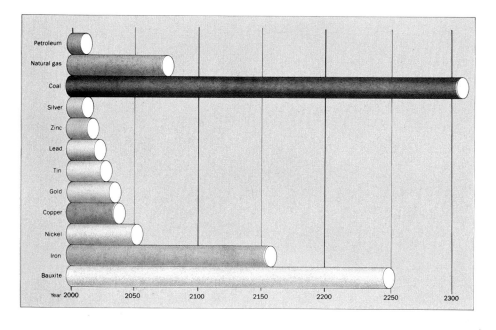

oil, coal, and natural gas. These do not renew themselves. Once a tankful of gasoline is burned, it is gone. The world will almost certainly run out of fossil fuels in the next few centuries, even if more deposits are located.

Price rises do most to reduce the use of fossil fuels, but few governments are willing to forfeit the taxes that they gain from people using their cars and other industrial products. More measures are desperately needed to conserve these resources.

Mining

People have been aware of the importance of minerals since prehistoric times. Access to metals that could be transformed into tools and weapons gave early peoples an advantage over their neighbors. The same demand exists today. Some minerals, such as bauxite, from which aluminum is made, are plentiful, but others, such as copper, lead, and nickel, are less so.

The developed world uses vast amounts of minerals. To extract them, huge ugly holes are dug in the ground, destroying the landscape and often ruining areas of outstanding beauty. The processes of refining metals usually create pollution of air and water. Efforts to control pollution, make mining more efficient, and relandscape despoiled countryside are made in many parts of the world. Industries also try to conserve metal reserves by reducing the amounts of metals they use and where possible by RECYCLING metals.

CONSERVATION FOR EVERYONE

Reduce, reuse, and recycle
Look at all your things. Do you need them? Did you need the packaging they came in? Did you throw it away, or did you find a way of recycling it? Take cans, bottles, jars, and old newspapers to be recycled. Don't make a special trip in the car to take small quantities of them, or you will use up more energy than you are saving. Never throw litter. It pollutes the streets and costs money for someone else to clear.

Switch it off
To make electricity, coal, oil, or nuclear fuel has to be burned. Try to save electricity. Turn lights off when you are not using them. Save heat by putting on an extra sweater or jacket when you are cold. Make sure there are no drafts around the windows and doors that let heat out. Hang the wash on the line for the sun to dry instead of using the dryer. Avoid washing single items in the washing machine or putting the oven on to heat one pizza.

Watch your water consumption
Some people have to carry all the water they need in containers from a river. Others simply turn on a tap and the precious liquid gushes forth. Do not fill your bath to the top. Use the bathwater or dishwater and put it on plants. Do not boil more water than you need. Never leave a faucet dripping. Put on a new washer.

Conserving our resources

We cannot leave the job of conserving the earth's resources solely to politicians, scientists, and industrialists. It is true that only they have the means to change conditions for the better where whole nations and even continents are concerned. Nevertheless, every day there are small, effortless ways in which individuals can help to improve the environment. We can conserve trees, minerals, and energy, reduce pollution, prevent waste, and generally improve the quality of life for everyone.

Because we lead busy lives, we often do not stop to think how our actions might affect the earth, or even if we do, cannot imagine that turning off a light or throwing away a piece of litter might improve or impair other people's lives. But they do.

A fit place for all

Each one of us can do much to make the world a healthier, safer place to live in. By understanding how the earth works, and how nature renews some resources but not others, we will better understand what changes it is sensible for people to make and what changes are harmful. We will learn how to prevent waste and use our resources for the benefit of everyone. We will learn how to conserve the land and farm it efficiently so that more people can be fed. We will prevent pollution so that our planet remains blue and beautiful.

Pass it on

Stop before you throw anything away. Open envelopes carefully so that you can reuse them. Give toilet roll tubes, empty plastic bottles, and egg cartons to the local school so that children can use them. Pass on toys and clothes that you have grown out of. Wear secondhand clothes instead of buying new. Keep plastic bags to reuse for shopping or throwing away garbage. Remember that what you think of as useless might be useful to someone less fortunate.

Make your garden grow

Grow your own vegetables and herbs in the garden. It will save you time shopping and cost you far less. Use yogurt containers for growing seedlings and cutoff plastic bottles to make mini greenhouses. Put vegetable peelings and organic waste on a compost heap.

Get on your bike

Do you need to take the car or the bus? Think before you do. Could you walk, cycle, or skate the distance? If you can, you will save gas, avoid creating fumes, and keep fit. If the distance is too great, choose the bus instead of the car. Public transportation solves traffic problems and congestion in towns, and helps cut down on pollution.

Arctic Ocean

The Arctic is a small, cold, shallow ocean around the North Pole. It is bordered by the northern coasts of North America, Asia, and Europe. The narrow Bering Strait links it with the Pacific. Several wider channels and the Norwegian Sea link it to the Atlantic. In winter the ocean is frozen, but in summer much of the ice breaks up.

Pacific Ocean

The Pacific lies between North and South America in the east and Asia and Australia in the west and stretches from the Arctic to the Antarctic, where it is linked to the Atlantic and Indian Oceans. North of the equator, it is the North Pacific, south of it the South Pacific. Its area is 64,000,000 sq. miles (166,000,000 sq.km.). It contains

OCEANS IN BRIEF

Surface area 139,700 sq. miles (362,000,000 sq. km.).
Average depth 12,795 ft. (3,900 m.).
Volume 323,900,000 cubic miles (1,349,900,000 cubic km.).
Pressure 14.9 lb./sq. in. (1.03 kg./sq. cm.) at the surface, increasing by that amount for every 33 ft. (10 m.) of depth. At 30,000 ft. (9,000 m.) pressure is 13,626 lb./sq. in. (939.5 kg./sq. cm.).
Deepest point 36,198 ft. (11,033 m.) in the Marianas Trench in the Pacific Ocean.
Average salinity 3.5 percent.
Highest tide 49 ft. (15 m.) in the Bay of Fundy, Canada.

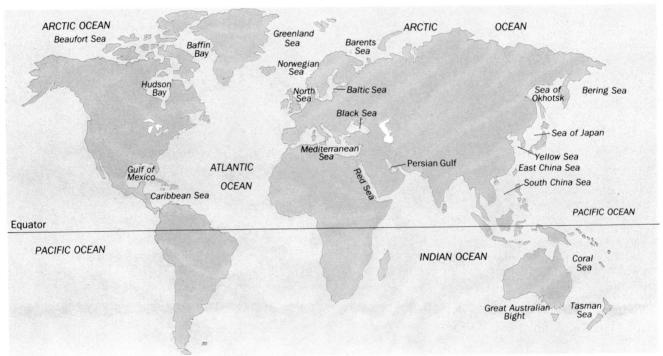

Atlantic Ocean

The Atlantic connects the two polar regions and is bordered by North and South America in the west and Europe and Africa in the east. It is fringed by several shallow seas, including the Caribbean, Mediterranean, and Baltic Seas. The area north of the equator is known as the North Atlantic; the area south of it, including the Antarctic area, is known as the South Atlantic. Second largest of the oceans, the Atlantic's area is 32,000,000 sq. miles (82,000,000 sq. km.), its average depth 10,800 ft. (3,300 m.). Running north-south through its length is a huge oceanic ridge, which rises as islands in several places. Iceland lies on the Atlantic oceanic ridge.

the deepest point so far measured, about 36,198 ft. (11,033 m.) in the Marianas Trench, and the highest underwater mountain, nearly 28,550 ft. (8,700 m.) near the Tonga Trench. It contains thousands of islands, many of them volcanic.

Indian Ocean

The Indian Ocean is bordered by the coasts of eastern Africa, southern Asia, and western Australia. It lies almost entirely south of the equator and is linked to the Pacific and Atlantic Oceans around Antarctica. It is linked to the Mediterranean Sea via the Red Sea and the Suez Canal. Third largest of the oceans, its area is 29,050,000 sq. miles (75,000,000 sq. km.).

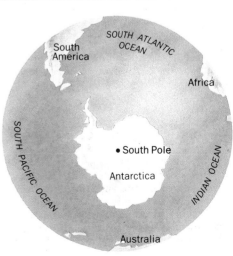

Continents

NORTH AMERICA

Land The Canadian Shield covers much of eastern Canada north of the Great Lakes. To the west lie the interior plains, which extend south between the Rocky Mountains and the Appalachians. West of the Rockies are other ranges, high plateaus, and basins. There are active volcanoes in southern Alaska, the northwestern United States, and Mexico. Most Caribbean islands are volcanic in origin.

Climate North America includes the world's second largest ice sheet (Greenland) and much of northern Canada has an Arctic climate. Much of the rest of North America has cold winters and warm summers. The interior plains are dry grasslands; deserts occur in the southwestern United States and northern Mexico. Central America and the Caribbean have a mainly tropical, rainy climate.

Plants South of the icy Arctic lands is treeless tundra. To the south are forests of conifers, which merge into mixed forests, containing such deciduous trees as maple and beech. Redwoods, cedars, firs, and

---

NORTH AMERICA IN BRIEF

Area 9,363,000 sq. miles (24,250,000 sq.km.).
Population 419,000,000.
Independent countries 23.
Mountain ranges Alaska, Appalachians, Cascade, Rockies, Sierra Nevada, Sierra Madre.
Rivers Mississippi-Missouri, Mackenzie-Peace, Yukon, St. Lawrence.
Lakes Superior, Huron, Michigan, Great Bear.
Islands Greenland, Baffin, Victoria, Ellesmere, and Newfoundland in the north. Cuba and other Caribbean islands in the south.

---

spruces grow in the northwestern United States, while hickories and oaks grow in the southeast. Tropical forests grow in parts of Central America.

Animals Caribou, polar bears, and seals live in the north. Forest animals include black bears, deer, and moose. The deserts contain rattlesnakes and many kinds of lizards. Alligators live in the southeast. The rain forests in the south contain many birds, monkeys, and jaguars.

People The first people were Amerindians, who arrived more than 20,000 years ago. From the early 16th century, Spaniards settled in Central America, where Spanish is now the main language. British and French people settled to the north. English

is the official language in the United States. French and English are official languages in Canada.

Economy North America is rich in natural resources; Canada and the United States are two of the world's richest nations. Mexico and the countries of Central America and the Caribbean are developing nations.

SOUTH AMERICA

Land The Andes mountains run for more than 4,900 miles (8,000 km.) through western South America. Many peaks are volcanoes. Many rivers, such as the Amazon and Orinoco, rise in the Andes.

Tributaries of the Amazon also rise in the Brazilian and Guiana Highlands. The Guiana Highlands contain Angel Falls, the world's highest. Broad plains lie to the east of the Andes in the south.

Climate The equator runs through the hot and wet Amazon basin. Deserts run down the west coast from Ecuador to northern Chile (the Atacama Desert). The Brazilian Highlands are hot and dry. Much of southern South America has a moist, temperate climate, but Patagonia is a cold desert.

Plants Tropical rain forest called SELVA covers much of the Amazon basin. Tropical grasslands lie to the north and south of the Amazon basin. The PAMPAS of Argentina

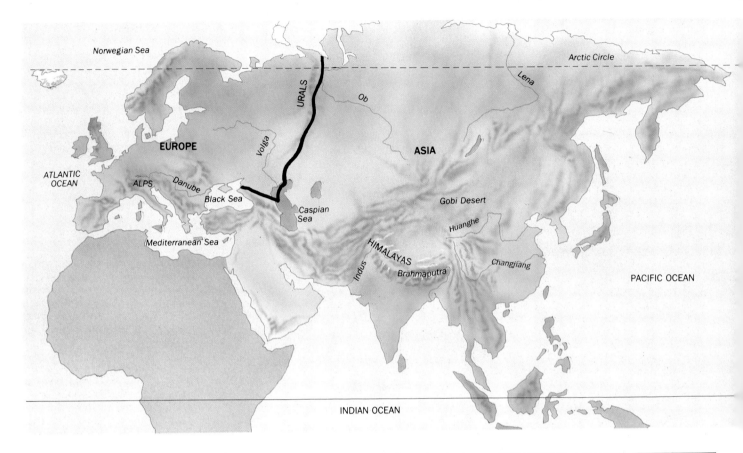

are temperate grasslands. The vegetation in the Andes varies according to the height, from tropical rain forest to peaks permanently covered by ice.

Animals The rain forests have a rich wildlife, including anacondas, anteaters, armadillos, capybaras, monkeys, and many kinds of birds. The vicuña and guanaco are found in the high Andes, together with llamas and alpacas.

People The first people were Amerindians, but in the 16th century Europeans seized most of the continent. Spanish is the official language in most countries, but Portuguese is spoken in Brazil. English is spoken in Guyana, Dutch in Suriname, and French in French Guiana.

SOUTH AMERICA IN BRIEF

Area 6,886,000 sq. miles (17,835,000 sq. km.).
Population 298,000,000.
Independent countries 12.
Mountain ranges Andes, Brazilian, and Guiana Highlands.
Rivers Amazon, Río de la Plata-Paraná, Madeira, Purus.
Lakes Titicaca in Peru and Bolivia.
Islands Tierra del Fuego, Falkland Islands (British), Galápagos Islands (Ecuador).

Economy South America is a developing continent, though Brazil and Argentina are expected to emerge as major powers in the next century.

EUROPE

Land East of the Scandinavian mountains in the north is the Baltic Shield, an area of ancient rocks and many lakes that makes up most of Sweden and Finland. Iceland, which is also part of northern Europe, is a young volcanic island. The Great European Plain runs from southern Britain across central Europe and includes most of the European part of Russia. The central uplands include low mountains and plateaus, including the Meseta of Spain and Portugal and the Massif Central in France. The Alpine mountain system includes not only the Alps but also the Sierra Nevada, the Pyrenees, the Apennines in Italy, the Balkans and Carpathians in eastern Europe, and the Caucasus range between Russia and neighbors Kazakhstan and Georgia.

Climate Northern Europe lies in the Arctic, but coastal areas are warmed by an ocean current called the North Atlantic Drift. This current gives west-central Europe a mild, moist climate, but conditions become increasingly severe to the east. The

---

EUROPE IN BRIEF

Area 4,066,000 sq. miles (10,530,000 sq. km.).
Population 696,000,000.
Independent countries 44.
Mountain ranges Alps, Apennines, Balkans, Carpathians, Caucasus, Pyrenees, Sierra Nevada.
Rivers Volga, Danube, Don, Rhine.
Lakes Caspian Sea, Ladoga.
Islands Great Britain, Iceland, Ireland.

---

warmest lands are in the south and the Mediterranean Sea is a major resort area.

Plants The north contains treeless tundra and coniferous forest. The former deciduous forests of central Europe have been cut down. The largest grasslands were in Ukraine and Georgia, but they are now largely used for crops. The Mediterranean region has much scrubland, called MAQUIS, with evergreens such as cork oaks and olive trees.

Animals Animal life has been much reduced by human activities. Brown bears and reindeer live in the north. The Alpine Mountains contain goatlike chamois and ibex. More common are such animals as badgers, moles, otters, rabbits, squirrels, and many kinds of birds.

People Europe is a densely populated continent, the home of the Greek and Roman civilizations, whose influence can still be seen. About 50 languages and many more dialects are spoken. Europe led the way in exploring and colonizing the world. Today several European countries have sizable groups of people of African and Asian origin.

Economy Europe's countries are highly developed, with many manufacturing industries and highly productive farms. As a result, most people enjoy high standards of living compared with those of people in developing countries.

ASIA

Land Asia, the largest continent, contains many mountain ranges, including the world's highest, the Himalayas. To the east and southeast is an island zone, stretching through Japan, the Philippines, and Indonesia, where the crust is unstable and volcanic eruptions and earthquakes are common. Asia also has some of the world's most densely populated river valleys and deltas. These contrast with the deserts of the southwest and center (the cold Gobi and Takla Makan Deserts). Another desert (the Thar Desert) is on the India-Pakistan border.

Climate The climate varies from bitterly cold Arctic conditions in the north to hot and steamy equatorial lands in the southeast. The southwest is hot and dry. Southern Asia is affected by monsoons—winds that blow from different directions according to the season. The summer monsoon in southern Asia often brings so much rain that floods occur.

Plants Asia has tundra and coniferous

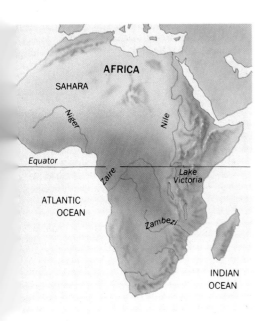

forests in the north and mixed and deciduous forests in the center. Dense tropical monsoon forest grows in the southeast, but plants are rare in the deserts.

Animals Foxes, lemmings, and reindeer live in the far north, while brown bears, lynxes, otters, and sables roam the northern forests. Southwest China is famed for the giant panda, but the greatest number of animal species live in the hot, wet lands of southern and southeastern Asia. They include crocodiles, rhinoceroses, and tigers. Camels, oryxes, and other animals live in the deserts.

People Asia was the home of early civilization and the birthplace of all the world's major religions. Today it has many ethnic, language, and religious groups. Each region has a distinct culture and its own characteristic political systems and tradi-

ASIA IN BRIEF

Area 16,970,000 sq. miles (43,950,000 sq.km.).
Population 3,202,000,000.
Independent countries 49.
Mountains Elburz, Himalayas, Karakoram, Tien Shan, Zagros.
Rivers Yenisey, Chiangjiang, Ob-Irtysh, Huanghe, Lena, Amur, Mekong, Ganges-Brahmaputra, Indus, Salween, Tigris-Euphrates.
Lakes Aral, Baikal, Balkhash.
Islands Borneo, Sumatra, Honshu, Sulawesi, Java.

tions. China and India are the world's two most populous nations. They contain about 37 percent of the world's people.

Economy Apart from Japan, one of the world's leading industrial powers, and part of Russia, most of Asia consists of developing countries, though some are rich in resources such as oil. But most Asians are poor compared with people in Europe and North America.

AFRICA

Land Most of Africa is a high plateau made of ancient shield rocks. The Drakensberg in South Africa is the uptilted rim of the plateau, but the highest peaks, Kilimanjaro and Kenya, are extinct volcanoes. East Africa contains the world's longest rift valley, which contains many lakes. Africa's long rivers are important for transportation, but near the coast (at the edge of the plateau) waterfalls and rapids make them unnavigable.

Climate Africa is a warm continent bisected by the equator. Between the warm

AFRICA IN BRIEF

Area 11,695,000 sq. miles (30,330,000 sq. km.).
Population 656,000,000.
Independent countries 53.
Mountains Ahaggar and Tibesti massifs in the Sahara; the folded Atlas Mountains; the Ruwenzori range in East Africa; and the Drakensberg in South Africa.
Rivers Nile, Zaire, Niger, Zambezi, Orange, Limpopo.
Lakes Victoria, Tanganyika, Nyasa, Chad.
Islands Madagascar.

Mediterranean regions in the north and far southwest (around Cape Town) are: hot deserts—the Sahara (the world's largest), the Somali, the Namib, and the Kalahari; tropical regions with wet and dry seasons; and equatorial regions, which are hot and wet throughout the year.

Plants The Mediterranean regions contain much scrubland, while few plants grow in the Sahara, except date palms around scattered oases. Tropical grassland (SAVANNA) is widespread, and rain forests grow in the hot, wet equatorial regions. The Kalahari in southern Africa has coarse grasses and scrub, while the interior of South Africa is VELD (dry grassland).

Animals Africa is rich in animal species, especially in the rain forests and savannas. Forest animals include chimpanzees and gorillas; crocodiles and hippopotamuses bask in the rivers. Savanna animals include buffaloes, elephants, giraffes, leopards, ostriches, and zebras.

People The two main groups are the Arabs and Berbers in the north and the black Africans of central and southern Africa. Until about 1960 most of Africa was ruled by European countries, but nearly all of Africa is now independent. The largest group of Europeans is in South Africa.

Economy Most African countries are poor and underdeveloped compared with those of Europe and North America, though Africa has many mineral resources. The rainfall is unreliable in many areas. Droughts cause crop failures and famines.

OCEANIA

Land Australia is an ancient landmass that has been so worn down that it is the flattest continent. The chief highlands are the Great Dividing Range in the east. Australia contains the world's largest coral formation, the Great Barrier Reef off the northeast coast. New Guinea is mountainous, with the region's highest peaks. New

PACIFIC OCEAN

INDIAN OCEAN

OCEANIA

GREAT DIVIDING RANGE

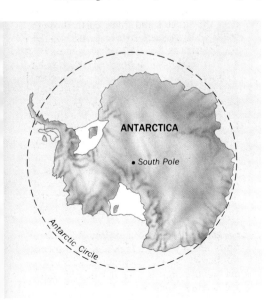

ANTARCTICA

• South Pole

Antarctic Circle

Zealand's Southern Alps are on South Island. North Island contains active volcanoes.

Climate Australia is the driest continent and much of western and central Australia is desert or semidesert. The sunny east and southeast coasts have ample rain and contain most of the country's population. Northern Australia and New Guinea have a tropical, rainy climate. New Zealand has a mild, moist climate.

Plants New Guinea has rain forests and tropical grassland. Savanna covers parts of northern Australia, while the west is largely desert or dry grassland. Acacias and eucalyptuses are common shrubs and trees. New Zealand has forests of evergreens and ferns.

Animals: New Guinea has many animals, including crocodiles, snakes, and brightly colored birds. Australia is famed for its marsupials, including kangaroos, koalas, and wallabies. Platypuses and echidnas are mammals that lay eggs. Many of New Zealand's animals have been introduced to Australia. Native species include reptiles called tuataras and many birds, including kiwis and keas.

People Most people in New Guinea are Melanesians. The aboriginal people of Australia settled there at least 40,000 years ago. But most Australians are descendants of immigrants from Europe, especially the British Isles. The Maoris of New Zealand are Polynesians, but most New Zealanders are of British origin. English is the official language in three countries of Australasia.

Economy Papua New Guinea is a developing country, but Australia, with its huge mineral resources, and New Zealand, famed for its agricultural exports, are both prosperous, and the people have a high standard of living.

ANTARCTICA

Ice and snow cover about 98 percent of Antarctica, the world's coldest continent. The ice reaches a depth of 15,750 ft. (4,800 m.), but in places mountain peaks appear through the ice. Mount Erebus, an active volcano, is on Ross Island. Wildlife is confined to the edges of the continent and includes penguins and seals. Whales swim in the surrounding seas. The only people are scientists who spend periods working there.

NORTH AMERICA

Arkansas Rises in the Rocky Mountains in the United States and flows east to join Mississippi River. Passes through Wichita, Tulsa, and Little Rock. Length 1,450 miles (2,334 km.).

Colorado Flows west from the Rocky Mountains in the United States to the Gulf of California. It has carved out the Grand Canyon in Arizona. Its vast Hoover Dam provides electricity for Los Angeles. Length 1,450 miles (2,334 km.).

Columbia Rises in the Canadian Rockies, flows south into the United States, and swings west to the Pacific. Its Grand Coulee Dam is the largest concrete structure in the world. Length 1,270 miles (2,044 km.).

Mackenzie Flows north from Great Slave Lake in Canada to the Beaufort Sea in the Arctic Ocean. It is frozen from October to June. Length 2,635 miles (4,216 km.).

Mississippi-Missouri Two rivers in the United States, which are usually considered a single system. The Mississippi rises near the Canadian border and flows south, to be joined at St. Louis by the Missouri, which rises in Montana. The Mississippi is the longest river in the United States, 2,348 miles (3,779 km.). The Missouri is second largest at 2,315 miles (3,726 km.). Together the rivers enter the Gulf of Mexico through an extensive delta. Their river basin is the third largest in the world. Length 4,663 miles (7,505 km.).

Missouri See Mississippi-Missouri.

Nelson This is the old fur trappers' route from Lake Winnipeg in Canada to Hudson Bay. Length 400 miles (644 km.).

Ohio Rises in the Appalachian Mountains in the United States and runs west to join the Mississippi at Cairo, Illinois. Fully navigable, it is important for freight. Pittsburgh and Cincinnati are on its banks. Length 981 miles (1,579 km.).

Potomac Historic river on which Washington, D.C. stands. Length 287 miles (462 km.).

Rio Grande Forms the border for 1,243 miles (2,000 km.) between United States and Mexico, where it is known as the Río Bravo del Norte. Flows into the Gulf of Mexico. Length 1,885 miles (3,034 km.).

St. Lawrence Flows from Lake Ontario in Canada to the Atlantic Ocean. The St. Lawrence Seaway, a system of canals, locks, and dams, has opened the way for seagoing vessels from Montreal to the Great Lakes. Forms border between Canada and United States for 113 miles (183 km.). Length 760 miles (1,223 km.).

Snake The major tributary of the Columbia River. Passes through Hell's Canyon, which is 125 miles (200 km.) long and up

Rivers of North America

Rivers of South America

to 7,900 ft. (2,400 m.) deep. Length 1,038 miles (1,670 km.).

Tennessee Largest tributary of the Ohio, with a system of dams that control floods, provide hydroelectricity, and make the river fully navigable. Length 652 miles (1,050 km.).

Yukon Rises in the Canadian Rockies and flows through Alaska to the Bering Sea. Icebound from October to June. Length 1,979 miles (3,185 km.).

SOUTH AMERICA

Amazon Rises in the Andes Mountains in Peru, 100 miles (160 km.) from the Pacific. Flows east across Brazil and into the Atlantic at the equator. The world's second longest river but easily the greatest; it contains a fifth of all the river water in the world. Its basin covers 2.7 million sq. miles (7 million sq. km.) and is the world's largest area of tropical rain forest. Length 4,000 miles (6,450 km.).

Colorado Rises in the Andes in Argentina. It flows east into the Atlantic through a delta south of Bahía Blanca. Length 530 miles (853 km.).

Madeira Third longest river in South America. Rises in Andes Mountains in Bolivia and flows northeast through tropical rain forest to Brazil, to join the Amazon near Manaus. Length 2,100 miles (3,380 km.).

Magdalena Rises in the Andes Mountains of Colombia and flows north into the Caribbean Sea through a wide delta. Length 1,000 miles (1,609 km.).

Negro Rises in northern Brazil and is a tributary of the Amazon, which it joins near Manaus. Its basin lies wholly in tropical rain forest. Its channel is more than 18 miles (30 km.) wide in places. Length 1,400 miles (2,253 km.).

Orinoco Chief river of Venezuela. It rises in the south and flows north along the Colombian border before turning east to the Atlantic. Length 1,600 miles (2,575 km.).

Paraguay Branch of the Paraná that rises in Brazil and flows south through Asunción, before joining Paraná. Length 1,500 miles (2,414 km.).

Paraná Rises in eastern Brazil, runs south and forms part of the border between Brazil and Paraguay. It flows on through Argentina to the Río de la Plata (River Plate) estuary and the South Atlantic. Its basin is the second largest in South America. Length 2,040 miles (3,283 km.).

Plata See Paraná; Uruguay.

São Francisco Rises in the Minas Gerais Province of Brazil and is the main route to eastern Brazil. Has third largest basin in South America. Length 1,800 miles (2,900 km.).

Tocantins Rises in central Brazil and flows north to Atlantic Ocean. Length 1,700 miles (2,736 km.).

Uruguay Rises in southern Brazil and flows south to join the Río de la Plata (River Plate). Forms part of border between Uruguay and Argentina and between Argentina and Brazil. Length 980 miles (1,577 km.).

AFRICA

Congo See Zaire.

Limpopo Also called the Crocodile River. Rises in South Africa and flows eastward, forming part of the border with Zimbabwe, through Mozambique and into the Indian Ocean. Length 1,000 miles (1,609 km.).

Niger Rises on the border between Sierra Leone and Guinea. It flows north and then sweeps south through Nigeria to its delta in the Gulf of Guinea. It is the third longest river in Africa and has the biggest delta. Length 2,600 miles (4,184 km.).

Nile The longest river in the world. It rises near the equator and flows north through the Egyptian desert to its huge delta on the Mediterranean Sea. Its two main branches are the White Nile, which starts at Lake Victoria in Uganda, and the Blue Nile, whose source is Lake Tana. The Blue Nile joins the White at Khartoum in Sudan. From there it is simply called the Nile. At intervals there are cataracts (rapids) and several dams, including the Aswân High Dam. Length 4,037 miles (6,497 km.).

Orange Rises in Drakensberg Mountains in Lesotho. It flows into South Africa and forms border with Namibia. It enters the Atlantic at Alexander Bay. Length 1,300 miles (2,092 km.).

Senegal Rises in Guinea in West Africa and flows north through Mali and then forms the border between Senegal and Mauritania all the way to the Atlantic. Length 1,050 miles (1,690 km.).

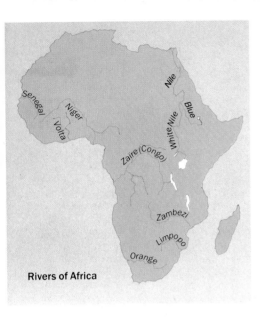

Rivers of Africa

Volta Rises in Burkina Faso and flows through Ghana into Gulf of Guinea at Ada. There are three arms: the Black, White, and Red Volta Rivers. The Akosombo Dam has created Lake Volta. Length 932 miles (1,500 km.).

Zaire (Congo) Forms part of the boundary between the countries of Zaire and Congo for part of its course and both names are used for it. Its chief headstream is the Lualaba. It drains the second largest river basin in the world. Length 2,900 miles (4,677 km.).

Zambezi Rises in northern Zambia and forms the border between Zambia and Zimbabwe. It flows into the Indian Ocean through a delta in Mozambique. Runs over the Victoria Falls. Length 1,650 miles (2,655 km.).

EUROPE

Danube Europe's second longest river, it flows from Germany through Austria, the Slovak Republic, Hungary, Serbia, Bulgaria, and Romania to the Black Sea. Length 1,725 miles (2,776 km.).

Dnieper Rises in the Valdai Hills near Smolensk in Russia and flows south to the Black Sea. Length 1,400 miles (2,253 km.).

Don Rises south of Moscow in Russia and flows into the Sea of Azov. Length 1,200 miles (1,931 km.).

Elbe Flows from its source in Czech Republic through Germany to the North Sea. Length 720 miles (1,160 km.).

Loire Longest river in France. It rises in the Massif Central and flows into the Bay of Biscay near Nantes. Length 625 miles (1,006 km.).

Northern Dvina Highly commercial river in northwest of Russia. Flows into White Sea near Archangel. Length 1,100 miles (1,770 km.).

Po Italy's longest river. It flows from the Alps to the Adriatic near Venice. Length 418 miles (673 km.).

Rhine The major waterway of western Europe. From its source in the Swiss Alps, it flows through Austria, becomes the border between France and Germany, and splits into a delta in the Netherlands, where it empties into the North Sea. Length 820 miles (1,320 km.).

Rhône Flows from Swiss Alps into France and south to the Mediterranean Sea. Length 500 miles (805 km.).

Seine Rises in central France and flows north, passing through Rouen and Paris, to the English Channel. Length 480 miles (772 km.).

Tagus Rises in Spain and flows through Portugal to the Atlantic. Length 566 miles (911 km.).

Thames From its source in the Cotswold Hills in England, flows past Oxford and through London to the North Sea. Length 209 miles (336 km.).

Volga The longest river in Europe. It rises in the Valdai Hills in Russia and flows through Volgograd to its estuary on the Caspian Sea near Astrakhan. Length 2,325 miles (3,742 km.).

ASIA

Amu Darya Rises in Pamir Mountains in central Asia and enters the Aral Sea

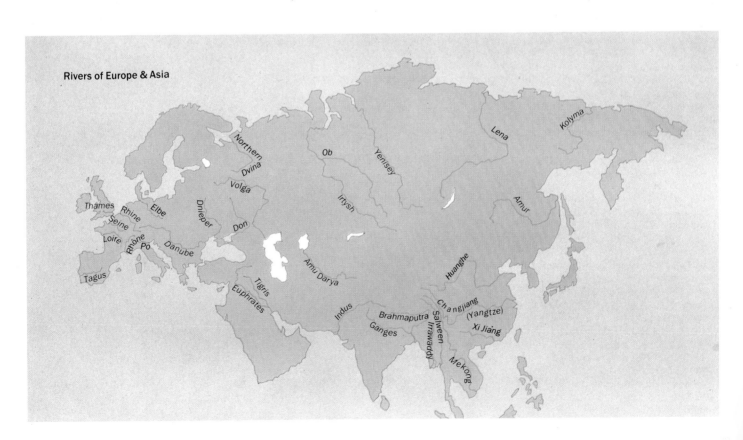

Rivers of Europe & Asia

Lakes

rivers of Australia & New Zealand

through a large delta. Its ancient name was the Oxus River. Length 1,400 miles (2,253 km.).

Amur Rises in northern Mongolia and flows into the Sea of Okhotsk. Forms border between Russia and China for almost 1,000 miles (1,610 km.). Its Chinese name is Heilong Jiang. Length 1,780 miles (2,865 km.).

Brahmaputra Flows from the Chinese Himalayas through India and Bangladesh into the Bay of Bengal. Forms an enormous delta with the Ganges. Length 1,680 miles (2,704 km.).

Changjiang (Yangtze) China's largest river and third longest in the world. It flows from mountains in southwestern China, through one of the most densely populated areas of the world, and empties into the East China Sea at Shanghai. Its basin covers nearly 20 percent of China. Length 3,100 miles (4,989 km.).

Euphrates Flows from eastern Turkey through Syria into Iraq. Joined by Tigris to form Shatt-al-Arab waterway before emptying into the Persian Gulf. Length 1,700 miles (2,736 km.).

Ganges River sacred to Hindus. Rises in Indian Himalayas and flows through densely populated areas of northern India and Bangladesh. It enters the Bay of Bengal through a massive delta. Length 1,550 miles (2,494 km.).

Huanghe (Hwang Ho) flows from western China to Bo Hai Gulf. Its name, which means "Yellow River," comes from the color of its silty water. It is also called "China's Sorrow" because of its frequent devastating floods. Length 3,000 miles (4,828 km.).

Hwang Ho See Huanghe.

Indus Rises in Tibet and flows south through Pakistan to northern Arabian Sea near Karachi. Length 1,800 miles (2,897 km.).

Irrawaddy Flows north-south through the whole length of Burma to delta on the Andaman Sea. Length 1,330 miles (2,173 km.).

Irtysh See Ob.

Kolyma Flows from the Kolyma Mountains of Siberia in Russia to the East Siberian Sea. Length 1,110 miles (1,786 km.).

Lena Longest river entirely in Russia. Rises near Lake Baikal in southern Siberia and flows to a delta on the Laptev Sea. Length 3,000 miles (4,828 km.).

Mekong Rises in Tibet and flows south through Laos, Thailand, Kampuchea, Vietnam, and enters the South China Sea through an extensive, marshy delta. Length 2,600 miles (4,184 km.).

Ob Rises in central Asia and, with its main tributary the Irtysh River (which flows from China through Kazakhstan into Russia) forms a vast river system. Flows into the Arctic Ocean. Length (Ob-Irtysh) 4,700 miles (7,580 km.).

Salween Rises in Tibet and flows through southern China and Burma into the Gulf of Martaban near Moulmein. Length 1,750 miles (2,816 km.).

Shatt-al-Arab See Euphrates.

Si Kiang See Xi Jiang.

Tigris See Euphrates.

Xi Jiang (Si Kiang) Rises in southern China and flows east to the South China Sea south of Guangzhou (Canton). Length 1,367 miles (2,200 km.).

Yangtze See Changjiang.

Yenisey Rises in central Siberia and flows north to the Arctic Ocean. Length 2,300 miles (3,701 km.).

AUSTRALIA AND NEW ZEALAND

Darling Tributary of Murray River in New South Wales and part of major irrigation and hydroelectric power schemes. Length 1,160 miles (1,867 km.).

Murray Australia's longest permanently flowing river. Rises in the Snowy Mountains in the Australian Alps and flows west into Encounter Bay. For 1,250 miles (2,000 km.) it forms the border between Victoria and New South Wales. Part of major irrigation and hydroelectric system. Length 1,200 miles (1,931 km.).

Waikato New Zealand's longest river. Flows northwest from the center of North Island to the Tasman Sea south of Auckland. Length 135 miles (217 km.).

Wanganui Rises in center of North Island and flows south into Tasman Sea. Famed for its beauty. Length 150 miles (241 km.).

NORTH AMERICA

Erie One of the Great Lakes, on the Canada-United States border. It receives water from Lake Huron via the St. Clair River, Lake St Clair, and the Detroit River, Lake St. Clair, and the Detroit River, while the Niagara River drains Lake Erie into Lake Ontario. The industrial cities of Buffalo, Cleveland, and Toledo are on the southern shore of Lake Erie. Area: 9,940 sq. miles (25,844 sq. km.).

Great Bear Lake Canada's largest lake and the fourth largest in North America. Part of the lake lies north of the Arctic Circle, and ice covers the lake for about eight months a year. The Great Bear River drains the lake into the Mackenzie River. Area: 12,000 sq. miles (31,200 sq. km.).

Great Salt Lake A lake in northwestern Utah that is saltier than the oceans. Its area often changes according to the flow of river water into it. Maximum area: about 2,328 sq. miles (6,030 sq. km.).

Great Slave Lake Lying in Canada's Northwest Territories, the Great Slave Lake is fed by the Slave River and is drained by the Mackenzie River. Area: 11,170 sq. miles (29,042 sq. km.).

Huron North America's second largest lake. In the north, St. Marys River connects it to Lake Superior, while the Straits of Mackinac link it to Lake Michigan. In the south, it drains into Lake Erie via the St. Clair River, Lake St. Clair, and the Detroit River. Area: 23,010 sq. miles (59,826 sq. km.).

Michigan The largest body of fresh water entirely within the United States, Lake Michigan is the third largest of the Great Lakes. The great industrial cities of Chicago and Milwaukee lie on its shore. Area: 22,400 sq. miles (58,240 sq. km.).

Nicaragua The largest lake in Central America, lying in western Nicaragua. It has several islands, some of which are active volcanoes. The Tipitapa River links Lake Nicaragua to Lake Managua to the north. Area: 3,060 sq. miles (7,925 sq. km.).

Ontario The smallest and most easterly of the Great Lakes, lying on the Canada-United States border. It receives water from Lake Erie through the Niagara River and is drained by the St. Lawrence River, which flows into the Atlantic Ocean. Area: 7,540 sq. miles (19,529 sq. km.).

Superior The most northerly and westerly of the Great Lakes, lying on the Canada-United States border. Lake Superior is the world's largest body of freshwater. Area: 31,820 sq. miles (82,732 sq. km.).

Winnipeg Lying in south-central Manitoba, Canada, Lake Winnipeg is one of the "Great Lakes of Manitoba," which was formed toward the end of the last ice age. Area of Lake Winnipeg: 9,460 sq. miles (24,596 sq. km.).

SOUTH AMERICA

Maracaibo South America's largest lake lies in northwestern Venezuela. A short, narrow channel connects it to the Caribbean Sea. Area: 6,300 sq. miles (16,380 sq. km.).

Poopó Situated in Bolivia, Lake Poopó is South America's third largest lake. It lies 12,093 ft. (3,686 m.) above sea level. Area: 1,004 sq. miles (2,600 sq. km.).

Titicaca The world's highest navigable lake, on the Bolivia-Peru border. Its shoreline is 12,507 ft. (3,812 m.) above sea level. Some local people live on floating islands made from reeds. Area: 3,200 sq. miles (8,300 sq. km.).

ASIA

Aral Sea A salty lake on Kazakhstan's border with Uzbekistan. The Aral Sea's area has been greatly reduced because water from rivers flowing into it has been used for irrigation. Area: about 15,483 sq. miles (40,100 sq. km.).

Baikal Lying in southeastern Siberia, Lake Baikal (or Baykal) is the world's deepest lake. It reaches a maximum depth of 6,365 ft. (1,940 m.). Area: 12,162 sq. miles (31,499 sq. km.).

Balkhash A lake in southeastern Kazakhstan. The water is salty in the east but fresh in the west. Area: 6,700 sq. miles (17,420 sq. km.).

Bratsk Reservoir An artificial lake in Siberia, on the Angara River. It has the greatest volume of water of any reservoir. Area: 2,112 sq. miles (5,470 sq. km.).

Caspian Sea The world's largest lake, it is bordered by Russia, Kazakhstan, Turkmenistan, Iran, and Azerbaijan. This salty lake has been shrinking because the rivers that feed it are used for irrigation. Area: 169,381 sq. miles (440,391 sq. km.).

Dead Sea Lying between Israel and Jordan in a deep rift valley, the Dead Sea is the world's saltiest body of water. At 1,286 ft. (392 m.) below sea level, the Dead Sea shoreline is the world's lowest point on land. Area: 370 sq. miles (962 sq. km.).

EUROPE

Constance Also called Bodensee, it lies on the borders of Austria, Germany, and Switzerland. The lake forms part of the course of the Rhine River. Area: 208 sq. miles (539 sq. km.).

Geneva Also called Lac Léman or Genfersee, it lies in a scenic region on the border between France and Switzerland. It forms part of the course of the Rhône River. Area: 226 sq. miles (585 sq. km.).

Ladoga Situated in northwestern Russia near St. Petersburg, Lake Ladoga is the largest lake that lies entirely in Europe.

Area: 7,000 sq. miles (18,200 sq. km.).

Onega A large lake in northwestern Russia that forms part of a waterway that links the Baltic and White Seas to the Volga River. Area: 3,764 sq. miles (9,786 sq. km.).

AFRICA

Bangweulu Situated in Zambia, Lake Bangweulu fills a shallow depression in the African plateau. It is one of the sources of the Zaire River (Congo). Area: 1,900 sq. miles (4,920 sq. km.), though heavy rains sometimes more than double its size.

Chad A large lake in North Africa on the Chad-Nigeria border. Since the 1970s, droughts have caused this shallow lake to shrink. Area: 6,293 sq. miles (16,300 sq. km.).

Kariba An artificial lake behind the Kariba Dam on the Zambezi River. Its hydroelectric station supplies electricity to Zambia and Zimbabwe. Area: about 2,007 sq. miles (5,200 sq. km.).

Malawi see *Nyasa*.

Nasser A lake on the Nile River in Egypt and Sudan. It was created by the Aswân High Dam in southern Egypt. Area: about 2,000 sq. miles (5,180 sq. km.).

Nyasa A lake in the Great Rift Valley between Malawi, Mozambique, and Tanzania. Area: 11,100 sq. miles (28,749 sq. km.).

Tana Situated in northwestern Ethiopia, it is the main source of the Blue Nile. Area: 1,418 sq. miles (3,687 sq. km.).

Tanganyika The world's longest and second deepest freshwater lake. It lies in the Great Rift Valley. It is 423 miles (680 km.) long and has a maximum depth of 4,708 ft. (1,435 m.). It is bordered by Burundi, Tanzania, Zambia, and Zaire. Area: 12,700 sq. miles (32,893 sq. km.).

Turkana A long, narrow lake, formerly called Lake Rudolf, lying partly in Kenya and partly in Ethiopia. Area: 3,500 sq. miles (9,100 sq. km.).

Victoria Africa's largest lake, situated in Uganda, Kenya, and Tanzania. It is the largest source of the Nile River. Area: 26,200 sq. miles (68,120 sq. km.).

Volta An artificial lake that has been formed behind the Akosombo Dam in Ghana. It is the world's largest reservoir in area. Area: 3,275 sq. miles (8,482 sq. km.).

AUSTRALIA AND NEW ZEALAND

Eyre Australia's largest lake, lying in north-central South Australia. For most of the time, Lake Eyre is dry. Area: 3,700 sq. miles (9,583 sq. km.).

Taupo New Zealand's largest lake, in central North Island, Lake Taupo is the source of the country's longest river, the Waikato. Area: 234 sq. miles (606 sq. km.).

Mountains

Names in *italics* indicate separate entries.

AMERICAS

Aconcagua Peak in Andes (Argentina), highest in South America, 22,830 ft. (6,960 m.).

Adirondacks Range in northeastern United States. Averages 3,900 ft. (1,200 m.) in height, with Mt. Marcy highest, 5,348 ft. (1,630 m.).

Alaska Range in southern Alaska that includes *Mt. McKinley*, the highest peak in North America.

Andes Range that stretches for over 4,000 miles (6,450 km.) down the western side of South America. In Bolivia and Peru, the Andes broaden into a plateau 370 miles (600 km.) wide and 13,000 ft. (4,000 m.) high. Formed by the collision of two plates, the Andes are mostly fold mountains. The plates are still moving and the Andes are still rising. Many peaks are over 19,000 ft. (6,000 m.) including the highest, *Aconcagua*.

Appalachian Group of mountain ranges in the United States that include the White and the Green Mountains, the Catskills, and the Great Smokies. They run for about 1,500 miles (2,400 km.) from the state of Maine in the north to Alabama in the south. Old fold mountains, they were uplifted between 250 and 500 million years ago. Once taller than the Himalayas, they have been worn down by millions of years of erosion. The highest peak is *Mt. Mitchell*.

Brazilian Highlands An upland region in east-central Brazil, mostly between 900 and 3,000 ft. (275 and 900 m.) above sea level. It forms a watershed between rivers flowing into the Amazon basin and other rivers flowing east and south into the Atlantic Ocean.

Cascade Range in United States stretching from northern California, through western Oregon and Washington, into southern British Columbia. Two volcanoes have erupted this century: Lassen Peak in 1921 and Mt. St. Helens in 1980. Highest peak is *Mt. Rainier*.

Cayambe Extinct volcano with square crater in Andes in Ecuador, 19,500 ft. (5,944 m.).

Chimborazo Extinct volcano in Andes in Ecuador, 20,561 ft. (6,267 m.).

Citlaltepetl (or Orizaba) Active volcano and highest peak in Mexico, 18,700 ft. (5,700 m.).

Cotopaxi Volcano in Andes in Ecuador. Long thought to be world's highest active volcano, 19,347 ft. (5,897 m.). The highest active volcano is now believed to be Ojos del Salado, 22,539 ft. (6,870 m.) on the Chile-Argentina border.

Elbert Highest peak of Rocky Mountains in Colorado 14,432 ft. (4,399 m.).

Lassen Peak See Cascade.

Logan Peak in Yukon in Canada. Highest peak in Canada and second highest in North America, 19,850 ft. (6,050 m.).

Mackenzie Range in northeastern Canada. Part of Rocky Mountain chain.

McKinley Peak in Alaska Range in United States. Highest in North America, 20,320 ft. (6,194 m.).

Mitchell Highest peak in Appalachians, in North Carolina, 6,689 ft. (2,037 m.).

Orizaba See Citlaltepetl.

Rainier Highest peak of Cascade Mountains in Washington State, 14,410 ft. (4,392 m.).

EURASIA

Alps Range in western Europe, up to 185 miles (300 km.) wide and about 745 miles (1,200 km.) long. They run from Slovenia to France, through Italy, Austria, Liechtenstein, Switzerland, and Germany. The Alps are fold mountains, uplifted during the past 25 million years as the African plate has pressed into the European plate. *Mont Blanc* is the highest peak.

Annapurna in the Himalayas in Nepal is the 11th highest peak in the world, 26,334 ft. (8,027 m.).

Ararat Volcanic mountain in Turkey. Sup-

Black Sea to the Caspian Sea. *Mt. Elbrus* is highest peak.

Communism Peak in Pamir Range in Tajikistan, 24,590 ft. (7,495 m.).

Elbrus Highest peak in Caucasus in Russia, and in Europe, 18,481 ft. (5,633 m.).

Etna Intermittently active volcano on Italian island of Sicily. Largest in Europe, 10,902 ft. (3,323 m.).

Everest Mountain in Himalayas, on Tibet-Nepal border. World's highest, 29,028 ft. (8,848 m.).

Fuji Dormant volcanic mountain on Honshu Island in Japan. Considered sacred by many Japanese, 12,388 ft. (3,776 m.).

Godwin Austen Mountain in Karakoram

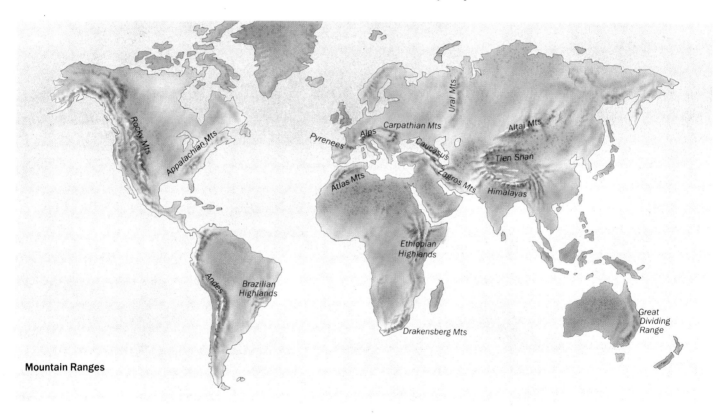

Mountain Ranges

Rocky Mountains System stretching for about 3,100 miles (5,000 km.) from Alaska in the north, down the western side of Canada and the United States. The Rockies consist of parallel ranges of high mountains with plateaus between them. In places the Rockies stretch 930 miles (1,500 km.) inland from the Pacific. They are mostly fold mountains that began to be uplifted about 70 million years ago. The highest peak in the Rockies is *Mt. Elbert.*

Whitney Highest peak in Sierra Nevada range in California. The highest peak in the United States outside Alaska, 14,495 ft. (4,418 m.).

posed resting place of Noah's ark, 16,945 ft. (5,165 m.).

Ben Nevis Extinct volcanic peak in Scotland. Highest in British Isles, 4,406 ft. (1,343 m.).

Carpathian Range running for about 800 miles (1,300 km.) from the Slovak Republic through Ukraine to Romania. They are fold mountains uplifted at the same time as the Alps. The highest peak, Gerlachovsky, is in the Slovak Republic, 8,710 ft. (2,655 m.).

Caucasus Range on border between Russia and Georgia and Kazakhstan, stretching for about 680 miles (1,100 km.) from the

Range of Himalayas in northern Kashmir. Also called K2. Second highest peak in world, 28,250 ft. (8,611 m.).

Himalayas Massive mountain system in central Asia, running from northern Pakistan, through northern India, Bhutan, and Nepal, to China. Range forms part of the largest and highest area of mountains on earth and includes *Mt. Everest*, the world's highest peak. Nearby ranges include the Hindu Kush, the Karakoram, the Siwalik, the Pamirs, the Chang Tang, and the *Tien Shan.* Tibet is a vast high plateau in the heart of the area. Glaciers are the source of many great rivers, including the Indus, the

Brahmaputra, the Ganges, the Changjiang, the Xi Jiang, and the Huanghe. The system began to uplift about 50 million years ago when the plate carrying India collided with the Asian plate. Enormously thick beds of rock that had been laid down between the two continents were folded, crumpled, and lifted when they met. Parts of the area are still rising.

Jungfrau Peak in Swiss Alps. Its name means "the Madonna," 13,642 ft. (4,158 m.).

K2 See Godwin Austen.

Kanchenjunga Peak in Himalayas on Nepal-Sikkim border. Third highest in world 28,208 ft. (8,598 m.).

Klyuchevskaya Highest of 18 active volcanoes in Siberia in Russia. Part of the "Pacific Ring of Fire," 15,577 ft. (4,748 m.).

Matterhorn Peak in Swiss Alps, 14,692 ft. (4,478 m.).

Mont Blanc Peak in France. Highest in European Alps, 15,771 ft. (4,807 m.).

Narodnaya Highest peak in Ural Mountains in Russia, at northern end of the range near the Arctic Circle, 6,214 ft. (1,894 m.).

Pyrenees Range some 267 miles (430 km.) long that divides France and Spain. They have been formed during the last 25 million years as Spain has been pushed against France by movements in the earth's crust. Highest point is the Pico de Aneto, 11,167 ft. (3,404 m.).

Snowdon Peak in Wales. Highest in England and Wales, 3,562 ft. (1,086 m.).

Stromboli Active volcano on island near Sicily in Italy, 3,038 ft. (926 m.).

Tien Shan Range in central Asia. The highest peak, on the China-Russia border, is Pik Pobedy (Tomur Feng in China), at 24,406 ft. (7,439 m.).

Urals Chain in Russia and Kazakhstan that forms part of boundary between Europe and Asia. The mountains run north-south for 1,490 miles (2,400 km.) between the Arctic Ocean and the Aral Sea. Like the Appalachians in North America, they were uplifted between 250 and 500 million years ago. Now of moderate height, they may once have been higher than the Himalayas. Highest peak is *Mt. Narodnaya*.

Vesuvius Active volcano near Naples in Italy. Numerous eruptions recorded. The most famous, in A.D. 79, destroyed Pompeii, 4,190 ft. (1,277 m.).

Zagros Range stretching from eastern Turkey through western Iran. It reaches 14,921 ft. (4,548 m.) west of the city of Esfahan.

PACIFIC

Mauna Kea Dormant volcano on island of Hawaii, 13,796 ft. (4,205 m.).

Mauna Loa Large active volcano on Hawaii, 13,680 ft. (4,170 m.).

AFRICA

Atlas Range in northwestern Africa. Ridges of fold mountains that run east-west for 1,491 miles (2,400 km.) through Morocco, Algeria, and Tunisia. Average height between 8,200 and 9,840 ft. (2,500 and 3,000 m.). Highest peak is Jebel Toubkal in Morocco, 13,665 ft. (4,165 m.).

Drakensberg Range in southern Africa. With Maloti Mountains, stretches through Lesotho and South Africa. Highest peaks are Thabana Ntlenyana, 11,423 ft. (3,482 m.) and Mont aux Sources, 10,823 ft. (3,299 m.).

Ethiopian Highlands Africa's most extensive mountain and high plateau region, rising to Ras Dashen, 15,158 ft. (4,620 m.).

Kenya Isolated extinct volcano in Africa, about 7 miles (12 km.) south of the equator in Kenya, 17,057 ft. (5,199 m.).

Kilimanjaro Isolated extinct volcano in Tanzania. Highest peak in Africa, 19,340 ft. (5,895 m.).

Ruwenzori Range of block mountains on the Uganda-Zaire border in Africa. The equator runs through the mountains and the snow line is at about 14,800 ft. (4,500 m.). Highest peak is Mt. Margherita, 16,763 ft. (5,109 m.).

AUSTRALIA AND NEW ZEALAND

Cook Mountain in Southern Alps on South Island. Highest in New Zealand, 12,349 ft. (3,764 m.).

Great Dividing Range System running north-south down eastern side of Australia, with various local names. The Snowy Mountains in the Australian Alps in New South Wales are highest in area and include *Mt. Kosciusko*.

Kosciusko Peak in Australian Alps in New South Wales. Highest in Australia, 7,316 ft. (2,230 m.).

Ngauruhoe Active volcano on North Island of New Zealand, 7,515 ft. (2,291 m.).

Ruapehu Active volcano on North Island of New Zealand, 9,175 ft. (2,796 m.).

Southern Alps Range of mountains running down western side of South Island, New Zealand. Mountains still being formed and subject to frequent minor earthquakes. Highest point is *Mt. Cook*.

Tongariro Active volcano on North Island of New Zealand, 6,516 ft. (1,986 m.).

ANTARCTICA

Ellsworth Highlands in Antarctica. Peaks stick up through ice sheet. Highest is *Vinson Massif*.

Erebus Antarctica's only active volcano, on Ross Island, 12,450 ft. (3,795 m.).

Vinson Massif Highest peak in Antarctica in Sentinel Mountains in Ellsworth Mountains, 16,863 ft. (5,140 m.).

Deserts

Major deserts appear on the map; there are many smaller deserts elsewhere, and there are individual deserts with local names within the larger areas. Names printed in *italics* indicate a separate entry.

AFRICA

Kalahari Covers 200,800 sq. miles (520,000 sq.km.) of southern Africa, mainly in Botswana. The land consists of barren red sand dunes and areas of scrub or semi-desert. A variety of animals, including big game, manage to live there. The original inhabitants of the desert, the Bushmen, live by hunting.

Namib Like the *Atacama* desert of South America, this is a narrow coastal desert where fogs are common and rain is infrequent. It lies mostly in Namibia and is virtually uninhabited.

Sahara The world's largest desert, it stretches 3,231 miles (5,200 km.) across North Africa and covers 3,200,000 sq. miles (8,300,000 sq.km.)—a quarter of the entire African continent. Only about one-tenth is sandy desert; the rest is bare rock or loose stones, and there are hilly and mountainous areas. Antelopes and other large animals live near water holes and oases, and in some places the nomadic Bedouin still follow their traditional ways of life. Once only camel caravans could cross the Sahara. Now, with the oil industry, travel by road is much easier.

Somali Inland desert in East Africa that covers 100,400 sq. miles (260,000 sq.km.), occupying most of Somalia and continuing across the border into Ethiopia.

ASIA

Arabian Eastward continuation of the *Sahara*. It stretches from the Red Sea, through Saudi Arabia, to Iran. In the north it includes parts of Jordan, Israel, Iraq, and Syria. In all it covers 500,000 sq. miles (1,300,000 sq.km.).

Gobi High plateau region in central Asia, which covers more than 386,000 sq. miles (1,000,000 sq.km.) of northern China and Mongolia. The desert is hot in summer, but the winters are long and bitterly cold. The few people who live in the desert are Mongolian nomads who herd cattle—longhaired yaks—and travel with camels. They live in warm tents called yurts.

Kara Kum (and Kyzyl Kum) West of the *Gobi* and *Takla Makan* Deserts and east of the Caspian Sea lie these two deserts, which are separated by the Amu Darya River. They cover an area of 200,000 sq. miles (520,000 sq.km.). Irrigation schemes allow crops to be grown in both deserts and for sheep, goats, and camels to be raised.

Takla Makan Desert in central Asia to the west of the *Gobi*. It lies between the Tien Shan and Kunlun mountains in China. It covers 174,000 sq. miles (450,000 sq.km.) and is mostly drifting sand dunes, which make its interior virtually uninhabitable. Temperatures are extreme, as low as 13°F (−25°C) in winter and as high as 86°F (30°C) in summer.

Thar Sandy desert that runs from northwestern India into Pakistan. Most of the desert is barren waste or scrub, but in some places there is enough rainfall to grow grass for grazing. Parts are also irrigated. There is one large town, Jodhpur, and many small villages.

hunting and gathering, and the inhabitants of isolated mining towns.

Individual deserts are the Great Sandy, the Gibson, and the Great Victoria.

AMERICAS

Atacama A narrow strip of land between the Andes and the Pacific Ocean in northern Chile is the driest desert on earth. It is claimed that parts of the Atacama had no rain for 400 years, from 1570 to 1971. The desert covers 69,500 sq. miles (180,000 sq.km.). Most of it is barren, but it is rich in minerals. A northern extension of the Atacama lies on the Pacific coast of Peru.

and New Mexico. Continuing south, the desert extends into Sonora and Baja California in Mexico.

Individual deserts in the region include the *Great Basin*, *Mojave*, Sonora, and Chihuahua.

Mojave Area in southeastern California that covers about 25,000 sq. miles (65,000 sq.km.) between the Sierra Nevada Mountains and the Colorado River. The vegetation is mainly desert scrub, consisting of creosote bushes and Joshua trees.

Patagonia This region near the tip of South America is partly in Chile and partly in Argentina. It covers about 297,000 sq. miles (770,000 sq.km.) and is a cold desert

Deserts of the World

AUSTRALIA

Great Australian This vast desert covers 600,000 sq. miles (1,550,000 sq.km.) in the center and west of Australia. An additional 560,000 sq. miles (1,450,000 sq.km.) is semidesert, making 1,160,000 sq. miles (3,000,000 sq.km.), which is about 39 percent of Australia. There are dried-up rivers and salt lakes.

Kangaroos and other marsupials can survive in the less barren areas. Rain is infrequent, but if enough falls the desert blooms as dormant seeds take root and flower.

Few people live in the desert apart from those aboriginal people who still live by

Great Basin Covers about 200,800 sq. miles (520,000 sq.km.), mostly in Nevada. The desert is surrounded by high mountains. Rivers flowing from the mountains dry up, leaving salt lakes that may be dry or wet. The Great Salt Lake is the largest.

Natural vegetation is scrub with a few trees. Death Valley, on the edge of the desert in California, is a desolate trough that contains the lowest land in the Western Hemisphere. The area is of spectacular beauty, rich in minerals and wildlife.

Great Western Once a vast area of the southwestern United States was barren land. Now, thanks to vast irrigation plans, much of the land is farmed and able to support industries and large populations in the states of California, Arizona, Texas,

plateau, similar to the *Gobi*. Only the valleys of rivers that rise in the Andes are fertile.

POLAR REGIONS

Arctic Around the Arctic Ocean at the North Pole there is a ring of cold lands. These frozen wastes cover parts of Canada, Alaska, Greenland, and Siberia. Mosses and lichens and low shrubs grow in snow-free areas, and flowers bloom in the brief summer.

Antarctica This roughly circular continent is larger than Europe and is so cold and barren that it can support no life except for a few plants around its edge.

Index and Glossary

Numbers in *italics* refer to illustrations.

Words in Roman type *in glossary entries refer to other entries in the glossary.*

Profiles of oceans, continents, rivers, lakes, mountains, and deserts are listed in alphabetical order on pages 78 to 89.